"I don't need a man in my life."

Gayle spoke stiffly. "And I don't appreciate being thought of as a sex object."

Jared smiled. "Maybe we should call it a scientific experiment. Bring Gayle Bradley Back to Life—that's a good motto. Maybe even teach her to play the field and enjoy it."

"I don't want to play the field!"

He looked her over, his eyes dark and appraising. "Why not?" he asked mildly. "Are you afraid you might find out you've wasted the past seven years? Or are you just chicken? I won't take advantage of you."

Her temper flared. "You couldn't seduce me if you tried!" she snapped. She saw the spark of satisfaction in his eyes, and only then did she realize she had issued a challenge.

LEIGH MICHAELS is married to "the best photographer in the United States," and in 1979 they published a photobook, *Pilgrimage,* documenting the Pope's visit to their home town of Des Moines, Iowa. She believes all good writing is actually rewriting and says if she could give one piece of advice to any beginning writer it would be this: "Nothing you have ever written is as good as it could be." She confesses to having sent a quarter of a million words up in smoke herself, but who's counting? Leigh holds a degree in journalism from Drake University and teaches a class now and then at the community college, usually in creative writing and journalism. Her family includes two teenagers, a cross-bred mutt who thinks he's human and a Siamese "aristo-cat." Leigh loves to write and has enough ideas for romances to keep her busy for a long time.

Books by Leigh Michaels

HARLEQUIN PRESENTS
702—KISS YESTERDAY GOODBYE
811—DEADLINE FOR LOVE
835—DREAMS TO KEEP
876—TOUCH NOT MY HEART

HARLEQUIN ROMANCE
2657—ON SEPTEMBER HILL
2734—WEDNESDAY'S CHILD
2748—COME NEXT SUMMER

These books may be available at your local bookseller.

Don't miss any of our special offers. Write to us at the following address for information on our newest releases.

Harlequin Reader Service
901 Fuhrmann Blvd.
P.O. Box 1325, Buffalo, NY 14269
Canadian address: P.O. Box 2800, Postal Station A,
5170 Yonge St., Willowdale, Ont. M2N 6J3

LEIGH MICHAELS

touch not my heart

Harlequin Books

TORONTO • NEW YORK • LONDON
AMSTERDAM • PARIS • SYDNEY • HAMBURG
STOCKHOLM • ATHENS • TOKYO • MILAN

Harlequin Presents first edition April 1986
ISBN 0-373-10876-1

Original hardcover edition published in 1985
by Mills & Boon Limited

CHAPTER ONE

THE building was quiet, except for the click of her heels on the polished marble floor as she crossed the lobby. She looked up at the arched ceiling, at the wrought iron panels of the balcony on the mezzanine floor, at the iridescent glass of priceless light fixtures, and thought about the contrast between the century-old building and the high-tech industry it sheltered. She shook her head. Only Logan Electronics would have dared to design sleek new computers in the elegant surroundings of another age.

The young man at the information desk looked up from his newspaper with a grin. 'Good morning, Miss Bradley. You're early. It's barely light outside.'

'I thought it was just dark because of the snowstorm coming in.' Gayle had scarcely noticed the still-dusky sky and the pale winter sun struggling to break through the morning haze. Her mind had already been at the office. A good executive secretary was a professional who didn't let things like weather or personal problems interfere with her job. And Gayle Bradley prided herself on being a professional.

The young man raised an eyebrow, but he didn't argue. 'You shouldn't worry so much about being on time,' he said, low-voiced, with a glance around the lobby to be sure no one could hear. 'It will be hours before Mr Logan comes down. On a morning like this, with Mrs Weston to entertain him, it will probably be noon before he comes out of the love nest.'

Gayle stopped dead her hand on the lift door. 'What did you call it?' she asked.

He winced, 'Sorry, Miss Bradley. That just slipped

5

out. But everybody knows about Mr Logan's penthouse and the——'

Gayle cut across his words. 'I don't believe that you're being paid to discuss Mr Logan's morals, Thomas.'

'Oh, come on, Miss Bradley,' he said, his tone a little defiant. 'You're not blind. You certainly know what goes on up there as well as anyone——'

'And I consider it to be none of my business. Mr Logan is my employer, and what he does with the rest of his time is not my concern.'

Thomas was abashed. 'Yes, Miss Bradley. But I can't understand why you're so blindly loyal to him.'

'Because he signs my paycheques, Thomas. You might think about that. I believe he still signs yours, too,' she added gently, and let the lift door close behind her.

Her cheeks were flushed, she saw in the long mirror on the elevator door. Embarrassment, for Jared Logan's sake? Hardly, she thought. But was Thomas right, when he said she was suffering from blind loyalty? It was a good question. She hadn't jumped to her employer's defence out of respect for the man, that was certain. She didn't even really like him, much less respect him. But when every employee in the entire building knew who was visiting him upstairs, it was time for someone to take a hand.

Obviously it would not be Jared Logan himself; he didn't care how public his affairs were. If Thomas were to ask Mr Logan about Natalie Weston and his love nest, the man would throw back his head and laugh— 'And pat Thomas on the head for being a good boy,' Gayle said crossly. 'Love nest—indeed!' It wouldn't exactly be the name she would choose for that penthouse apartment atop the Logan Building—she could think of a few adjectives that were far more appropriate.

She was still scowling when the lift reached the

eighteenth floor. She unlocked the door of the office suite and simply stood there for a long moment, her irritation at Jared Logan forgotten. The sweep of glass before her, with its ever-changing panorama of the city skyline and the foothills of the Rocky Mountains beyond, never failed to take her breath away. Today, the sky was low and sullen, with the promise of snow, and the foothills were hidden by the grey clouds. But the beauty that was Denver was always there, just outside her window. And on every new day, it was different.

Gayle hung her wool coat in the closet, made sure every dark brown strand of hair remained smoothly in the neat coil at the back of her neck, straightened her cuffs and the skirt of the black dress. She always wore black in the office—well tailored and good quality, severely plain and just a shade longer than the prevailing style. It was her uniform, part of being a professional who sought no attention for herself. A good secretary faded into the background and left the honours for her boss.

Her first action, as it was every morning, was a quick tour of the office suite, making certain that the cleaning woman had left everything in order. She straightened the blotter on the inch-thick plate glass table that Jared Logan used as a desk, started a fresh pot of coffee, turned on his personal computer, opened a new package of pencils and sharpened three to needle points. It was all done automatically, with the ease of two years of practice, while her mind was somewhere else.

Had it really been so long, she wondered, since she had come to work here? Two years of her life, spent in the executive suite at Logan Electronics, and she still didn't know her fellow employees any better than the day she had first walked into that coldly beautiful marble hall downstairs, on her way to the job interview.

That's exactly how you want it, she reminded herself

curtly. Gayle didn't intend to get involved with anyone
or anything. She would take care of herself and let the
rest of the world go by. It was a choice she had made
years ago, for even friendship caused hurt, and she
didn't intend to be hurt again.

'Enough of this nonsense,' she told herself. 'You're
sounding like a wish-washy little girl—changing your
mind about things that were decided long ago.' She put
it firmly out of her mind and sat down at her own desk
to tackle the problems of the day.

The new advertising mock-ups had come up—the
advance copies of an ad campaign that would begin
within the next few weeks, when Logan Electronics'
brand-new computer, the latest of a long line, would be
released. Gayle pulled the glossy photos out of the
portfolio and spread them out on her desk.

The ad manager had taken advantage of the very
contrast which had been in Gayle's mind that morning,
and so the new computer had been photographed down
in the grand foyer, with the gleam of old marble
reflecting around it.

It was a well-conceived, well-carried out plan. The
photography was superb; the contrasts were sharp and
eye-catching. And the model had been well-chosen, too,
Gayle had to admit. Natalie Weston, in an ante-bellum
ball gown with a frilly parasol, played the astonished
belle who had stumbled across this unknown, sleek
machine. She looked wonderful.

Gayle flipped through the photographs. Natalie was
thoroughly professional when it came to modelling, but
even she had been worn out by the ad manager's
demands for perfection this time. One of the glossy
colour photos had caught her hamming for the camera,
in a sultry movie-star pose with her hoopskirt caught up
at an angle no southern belle would ever have been
caught dead in.

Gayle looked at the photograph for a long time,
wondering why on earth the ad manager had included

it—it certainly would never appear in a magazine!—and whether she should take it out before the boss saw it. Would Jared Logan laugh, or would he scold the ad manager for wasting his time? It was so difficult to anticipate him, she thought, even after two years ... And if Natalie Weston was indeed the woman in the penthouse today—there was no way of knowing how Mr Logan would react to that less-than-tasteful photo.

In the end, she left it in the portfolio. It wasn't her business to censor what Mr Logan saw. But she made a mental note to talk to the ad man. If he was merely trying to add a little humour, Gayle thought he should be warned that he was treading on thin ice.

It was only an hour later when Jared Logan came in. So much for Thomas' ability to predict the boss, Gayle thought drily. It was certainly no better than her own.

'Good morning, Miss Bradley,' he said briskly, without looking at her, and went on into his own office.

She followed him, notebook in hand, and sat down silently by his desk. He poured his coffee into a big mug, ran a hand over the surface of the new computer as if he found in it a sensual experience, and pulled the leather chair around to face her.

He was as elegantly tailored this morning as ever, she thought, and felt again just a little of the shock she had experienced when she first met Jared Logan. She'd been told only that he built computers, and she'd come to her job interview expecting a long-haired, bearded, wild-eyed kid who spoke computer jargon rather than English. Instead, she had found a man who wore silk shirts and hundred-dollar ties, who played as hard as he worked, who indulged himself in a small dark moustache but kept it neatly trimmed—She suddenly realised that she was staring at him, and dropped her eyes to the notebook in her lap.

'Will I pass inspection this morning, Miss Bradley?' he asked quietly.

Gayle looked up, feeling an irrational desire to

puncture that self-satisfied air of his. 'You could use a haircut,' she said.

Jared Logan's hand went automatically to the dark brown hair at the back of his neck. The gold Liberty dollar in the heavy ring on his finger gleamed under the office lights. He looked startled.

Satisfied at her advantage, Gayle asked sweetly, 'Shall I make an appointment for you?' A man might be all-powerful, she reflected. He might even be a god to his wife, if he had one, which Jared Logan didn't. But he had no secrets from his secretary.

He watched her for a long moment, like a cat who was considering pouncing. Then he smiled, and his midnight-blue eyes sparkled. 'Your point, Miss Bradley.'

Gayle said calmly, 'I don't know what you mean, Mr Logan.'

'Shall we get down to business?' The humour had died out of his face. 'The new ad campaign was supposed to be here this morning,' he grumbled.

Gayle reached across the desk and handed it to him. 'I also have the Softek files out for you to review before you leave tonight,' she said.

'Good, I want to have everything at my fingertips when I go talk to Russell Glenn,' He opened the portfolio and glanced at the top photograph.

'If you'd like, I could arrange to be here in the office this weekend, in case you need more information,' Gayle offered.

He looked up in surprise, 'You'd give up a whole weekend, just on the off chance I might call?'

She didn't like the way he'd said that, she thought. He made it sound as if she would be sitting by the 'phone like an anxious teenager, waiting for a new boyfriend to call. She shrugged. 'It's part of my job,' she said quietly. 'And there are plenty of things that need doing around here.'

He turned back to the photographs. 'It won't be

necessary, Miss Bradley. I don't expect that we'll come
to an agreement this weekend, anyway. He says he
wants to sell Softek, but it's waited all these weeks. It
can wait another three days.'

Gayle nodded. She'd been in on this negotiation for
months, since Logan Electronics had made the first
tentative approach to buying the computer programming company that would double the services it could
offer to customers.

'What I can't figure,' he mused, 'is why Russ is
holding out. That one division based here in Denver,
when the rest of his holdings are in California, makes
no sense at all. I can't understand why he hasn't jumped
at the chance to sell it before it causes him trouble.'

Gayle didn't comment. He hadn't expected her to
answer, she knew; he had only been thinking aloud. She
glanced down at her notebook, at the list of messages.
'Peters called this morning and asked if you wanted him
to pack you things for the weekend.'

'I'll call him.' He didn't sound interested. He was
flipping through the photographs as he listened, and
now he stopped to look more closely at one.

'He also wanted to know if you'd be coming to Pino
Reposo before you left, or if he should bring your
luggage to Denver.' She kept her voice carefully neutral.
'He said it had been quite a while since he'd seen you.'

Jared looked up. 'You needn't pass on the message
word for word, Miss Bradley. I'm quite aware of what
my houseman thinks of me.' He pulled a single
photograph out of the pile, set it face down on the
corner of his desk, and pushed the rest back into the
portfolio. 'Tell Ron these are fine. He can use any of
them. And ask him when I can see the television spots.'

'He said they'd be ready next week.'

'Good. We need to get started on the arrangements
for the sneak preview party. It's only three weeks away.'
He was getting restless, she saw, his long fingers
wandering over the glass surface of the desk, reaching

for the computer as if he couldn't wait another instant to play with it. 'Oh, please send two dozen roses—yellow ones, this time—to Mrs Weston. She's staying at the Brown Palace.'

Gayle nodded and made a note. She didn't trust herself to speak. He often said it with flowers—but usually he confined himself to a dozen. Natalie Weston must be something special.

He must have seen the frozen look on her face, because his hands stilled suddenly. 'You and Peters agree, don't you Miss Bradley?' he said. 'Neither one of you thinks much of me.'

She kept her eyes on the lined page of the notebook. 'It isn't my business to think about you at all, Mr Logan,' she said woodenly. 'If that's all this morning, I'll go back to my work.'

He waved a hand towards the door, and silently, Gayle went out.

The promise of snow had been fulfilled, and the bus laboured through the streets at dusk that night. Gayle glanced at her watch and wondered if Jared was flying towards California to meet with Russell Glenn or if his plane was stranded on the ground at Stapleton International. As lucky as he is, she thought, he's probably well on his way towards sunshine and seacoast, while the rest of us are struggling with winter. And wait and see, she grumbled, even if he spends all weekend arguing with Russell Glenn, he'll manage to come back on Monday afternoon with a tan that looks like a month in the Bahamas.

She sighed and stood up as her bus came to its stop. Thank heaven her brother had been sensible enough to buy a house just a block from the stop. Otherwise, Gayle would have gone straight home to her apartment and called him to say that she couldn't possibly make it for her regular Friday night dinner with Darrel and Rachel and their little daughter.

It was with relief that she saw Darrel at the door as she came up the sidewalk. 'I was watching for you,' he greeted, pulling her into the warmth of the house. 'I didn't realise the snow was so bad, or I'd have come after you.'

'If the bus was having trouble, how could you have managed with that little car?' She gave him a hug. 'It smells wonderful in here.'

'It's ravioli night,' Rachel announced from the kitchen door. 'I've spent all week playing with the pasta machine you got me for Christmas.'

'In that case, I know it was the right choice.' Gayle let Darrel hang up her coat and followed Rachel back to the kitchen, rubbing her wind-reddened cheeks. In the middle of the kitchen floor, little Amy, who was three, was absorbed in a colouring book. She looked up, flung her crayon aside, and bounced across the room to Gayle, demanding to be picked up.

'Five place settings?' Gayle asked. 'There are only four of us.' She dropped a kiss on Amy's brunette curls and shifted the child to a more comfortable position.

Rachel pulled a loaf of garlic bread out of the oven. Her cheeks were flushed. 'One of Darrel's friends is coming over,' she said with a careless shrug.

Gayle wasn't fooled. 'Rachel, we've been through this before. You know I'm just not interested in meeting anyone now——'

'Or ever, apparently. It's been years, Gayle, and you don't seem to care if you never meet another man.'

'There are none who come up to my standards.'

'Honey, believe me, there would be if your standards were a little more realistic. I know a hundred men who would love to date you——'

Gayle sat down, settling Amy on her lap. 'So what does this one have that the other ninety-nine don't?'

Rachel turned to her with a brilliant smile. 'I knew you'd start being reasonable someday. For one thing, he has his own business. He's thirty-five——'

'Married?'

'Of course not! Would I set you up with a married man?'

Gayle looked her over thoughtfully. 'How long has he been divorced?'

Rachel sighed. 'Just about a year, Gayle, you can't expect to find this perfect man just sitting there waiting for you at the bus stop some morning, having appeared out of thin air. Any man you date is going to have a past——'

'Does he have any kids?'

'Three,' Rachel admitted reluctantly. 'But his ex-wife has custody.'

'Rachel, really.'

'It's no sin to have kids, for heaven's sake. You like Amy well enough . . .' Rachel directed a pointed look at her daughter, snuggled on Gayle's lap.

'It's different. I love taking care of Amy. I'm a wonderful aunt. But to be a stepmother . . . No, thanks.'

'Just what is it you want Gayle?'

'To be left alone! I like my life just the way it is. I like my job and I'm making plenty of money to take care of myself—I don't need a man!' Her words echoed vehemently.

Rachel's eyes were sympathetic. 'Aren't you lonely sometimes?'

'So is everyone else—sometimes. Rachel, you knew Craig. After loving him and losing him, it would take a superman to make me forget him.'

'I'm not asking you to forget him, just to go on with your life. Damn it, Gayle, the man's dead! It isn't as if you were married to him——'

She broke off when she saw the set look on Gayle's face, and knew that she had gone too far. 'Sorry,' she added cautiously. 'I only want to see you happy, Gayle. But I don't know anyone who wears a red cape and leaps tall buildings in a single bound. I'm doing the best I can.'

Gayle had to laugh. But her voice was firm as she said, 'I'll do my own looking, Rachel, when and if I'm ready. And if you ever greet me with an unexpected guest here again, I'll walk out.'

Rachel nodded unhappily. 'As long as you stay to meet Larry tonight, I promise I'll never do this again.'

Gayle felt suspicion rising. 'That promise certainly came easily,' she mused. 'Are you so sure that this is the one and only man for me?' Rachel didn't answer, and Gayle finally said, 'All right, I'll stay. But only because it's snowing, and the ravioli smells so good.'

It didn't take long to regret the decision. Hell would be a picnic, Gayle thought irreverently midway through the evening, compared to spending a lifetime with Larry. He was nice enough, and he obviously liked her. But something in her shuddered away from his touch. It wasn't only a physical thing, she concluded, trying to puzzle out the odd way she felt. She didn't want him to touch her mind, either. She didn't want to share her thoughts, or talk about the things that were essential to her. Perhaps it was selfish of her, she thought, but Larry simply would not understand. Not as Craig had understood her every thought almost before it was uttered . . .

The pain that she had thought long-buried came back, wracking her with its very unexpectedness. She had learned, over the years, to cope with it, to expect it on his birthday, or the holidays—but she had not seen this one coming, and it almost devastated her.

Rachel saw its reflection on her face, and was frightened. 'Gayle?' she breathed.

'I'll be all right.' Gayle forced a smile. 'I think the snow has let up, and I really must go home. It's been a long week.'

'I'll take you,' Larry volunteered, and Gayle could have kicked herself for not anticipating his offer.

'No, I'll call a cab. It's out of your way, and on a

night like this——' But her protest was futile, and before she realised what was happening she was bundled into her coat and scarf and sitting in Larry's car.

'Let the cabbie have a night off,' he said comfortably. 'I'm used to driving in this stuff.'

The snow had stopped. In the cloudless sky, a few of the brightest stars outshone the city lights below. Despite the hour, the ploughs were running, pushing the heavy snow aside to let traffic resume its normal flow.

As the car pulled up in front of Gayle's apartment, she sneaked a look at her wristwatch. Not late enough to plead exhaustion, she decided, and after all the man had driven across town on nasty streets to bring her home . . .

'Would you like to come up for coffee?' she asked.

His shy smile sent shivers up her spine. Perhaps she was being a little hard on Larry, she thought. It wasn't his fault that he wasn't Craig.

As she turned on the light in her apartment, she looked around it with suddenly new eyes. The comparison to the cheerful suburban clutter of Rachel's house struck her hard. Here everything was in place. Every book was straight on its shelf. Every print was square on the wall. Each cushion on the couch was fluffed and neat. There was not a toy, not a speck of dust—not a single human thing, she thought, and then shook the thought out of her head. How utterly silly that thought was! The entire apartment reflected her taste, her way of living. It had taken years to get it just the way she liked it.

'Nice place.' Larry was looking at the Salvador Dali print above her fireplace, one of a numbered series, as if he'd like to scratch his head in puzzlement. And that print, Gayle thought, was one of the artist's more realistic works. What would Larry think if she'd had one of the surrealistic ones on her wall?

She went on to the kitchen and started the coffee.

'What is this thing supposed to be?' he called.

'Do you mean the Dali?'

'It doesn't look like a doll to me.'

'Not a dolly, Dali—the artist.' Gayle gave up. She wasn't about to start a course in art appreciation at this hour.

He came to the kitchen a few minutes later. 'You really did mean coffee,' he said.

'Of course. What did you think I meant?' Gayle knew that she sounded a little cross, and she didn't care.

'Sometimes a girl means other things,' he said obliquely.

Gayle set a mug on the countertop, hard. 'Such as an invitation to stay the night? I've only known you five hours, Larry.'

He shrugged. 'It's okay by me. I'm easy to please.'

'Well, I'm not. So you can either stay for coffee or you can get out of here, but I want it clear that coffee is all you're getting.'

He picked up a mug and held it cupped in his big hand, his eyes pleading. 'Not even a cookie?' he asked finally.

'Not even that.' He looked so much like a wounded puppy that she would have liked to throw him a bone. But, like a puppy, a scrap would probably only encourage him to hang around and wait for another feeding, she thought.

They drank their coffee in almost total silence. Without Darrel and Rachel to ease the conversation, there was nothing to talk about. It was with relief that she saw him to the door, offered her hand to shake rather than her cheek to be kissed, and said goodbye. As soon as he was gone, she leaned against the door, knees weak, and closed her eyes in silent thankfulness that the evening was finally over.

A weekend of blessed solitude stretched before her. Two glorious days in which she needed to answer only to herself. She would go to the art museum, she decided. And perhaps that little gallery where she had bought the Dali print—her bank account would stand another purchase now. And she'd drink hot chocolate and walk in the snow—and by Monday she'd be ready to face the world again.

CHAPTER TWO

LARRY called her three times on Saturday. She didn't know how many other times he'd tried, but he caught her once just as she was getting into the shower, once as she was on her way out the door, and once in the middle of a facial mask that tightened her skin so much that she couldn't talk plainly enough to tell him what she thought of him. After that, she simply unplugged the telephone. No one else was likely to call, she thought.

It felt a bit like being a prisoner, and when she stepped out into the cold crispness of Monday morning on her way to the office, it was a welcome release to freedom. She took a deep, grateful breath of the oxygen-thin high altitude air, and noted that it was going to one of the clear, cold days that she loved so well—days that left her skin tingling and fresh.

'Gayle!' The shout came from a car parked in front of the apartment building, and her heart sank. So much for the lovely day, she thought.

'Good morning, Larry,' she said, trying to keep her temper.

'I was driving by on my way to work and thought I'd stop and see if you'd like a ride.'

'No, thanks. My bus will be along in a minute.'

But he took her arm. 'I tried to call, but your 'phone just rang and rang. I thought you weren't home, but I decided it was worth a try, so I stopped.'

'Larry, my bus——'

'Nonsense, I'm driving right by your office.'

Before she could argue further, she found herself in the passenger seat. On Friday night it had been too dark, and she had been too nervous about the streets, to pay attention to his car. Now she was a little surprised to realise that it was a nice one, a luxurious late model. But then Rachel had said that he was well-off, that he owned his own business . . .

And it didn't matter a darn, either. Larry could be the richest man in the whole state and it wouldn't change her mind. It wasn't that she had anything against Larry, really, Gayle told herself. Even his persistence would be rather flattering, if she wanted to be pursued. But she didn't. She just didn't want to get involved with anyone.

Now if she could only find a way to tell Larry that, without hurting his feelings!

'Would you like to meet me for lunch?' he asked. 'I'll be around the downtown area most of the day, and I could . . .'

'No.' It was a bald statement, and Gayle tried to soften it up. 'I seldom leave the office at lunchtime. There is always something to do.'

He shook his head. 'That's not good for you, skipping meals. What about dinner, then?'

'Not tonight,' she said, and could have bitten off her tongue when she realised that she'd implied that any other night would be just fine. 'My boss will be back today, and that always means staying late.'

'Then you really should have lunch. What if I——'

'No, Larry.' She was beginning to sound cross. What a way to start a week, she thought.

He drove slowly, as if he was reluctant to let her go, and by the time the car pulled up in front of the Logan building, Gayle was fretting. She hadn't been late to work in a year, and if this clown caused he to be tardy today . . .

Then she told herself to relax. Jared Logan's plane wasn't due in till afternoon, and nobody else would care whether she was at her desk precisely on the dot.

Larry stopped the car and leaned across her to open the door. 'Can I call you at the office later on, or does your boss frown on that too?'

Gayle seized her opportunity. 'He hates personal calls on his time, Larry. I could lose my job.'

He smiled comfortingly. 'Don't worry about it, little lady. From what Darrel tells me, a high-powered woman like you could get a job anywhere. As a matter of fact, I could use a good secretary, myself. But don't worry. I'll just call you at home tonight.'

Gayle pushed the car door open and stepped up to her knees in a snowbank at the kerb. A word she seldom used came to her lips as she struggled through the snow to reach the cleared sidewalk.

'Miss Bradley, I'm shocked at you,' a mild, deep voice said at her elbow. A hand in a dark-brown leather glove set the revolving door in motion, and Gayle was through it and into the lobby before she recovered herself.

'What are you doing back so soon?' she accused.

'Were you plotting a coup in my absence?' Jared Logan countered.

'Of course not. But I didn't think anything could get you out of the sunshine a minute sooner than necessary.'

'On the contrary. I came home Saturday.' He looked tired, as if the fast trip had drained his strength.

Or perhaps, Gayle thought cattily, Natalie Weston had been more demanding than usual last night. If indeed it was still Natalie, and not some new charmer—an airline flight attendant, perhaps. Oh, well, she thought. She'd know soon enough—when he told her where to send the flowers.

He was watching her speculatively, as if wondering what she was thinking. 'I spent the rest of the weekend at Pino Reposo,' he announced. 'So you and Peters can stop reminding me of how long it's been since I spent any time there.'

Gayle nodded a greeting to Thomas, who was on his best behaviour at the information desk. Then she stepped into the lift and leaned against the wrought iron grillwork.

'It was almost exactly a month,' she pointed out, addressing the mirrored ceiling as the lift creaked into action. 'What I don't understand is this—why do you keep the place if you don't like it?'

'I love it. It's just too far from Denver.'

'Then why not sell it and find something closer?'

'Why should I? I have the best of both worlds—the penthouse here so I can be close to my work, and Pino Reposo so I can retreat from the world.' The name rolled from his tongue.

'Pine Rest,' she murmured. 'It sounds so much better in Spanish, especially when you say it.' In fact, she thought, with his dark hair, heavy tan, and moustache, he looked a little like a caballero himself.

'Miss Bradley, you sound almost like a romantic.'

She smiled. 'Don't kid yourself, Mr Logan.'

The lift gave a sudden lurch, and Gayle's stomach protested just as it always did on a roller coaster. Then the lights died, the ventilating fan went off, and the lift hung unmoving in the shaft.

'What the devil!' Jared said. 'I intended to put an override system on these damned antiques, and I never got around to it.'

'It probably wouldn't have mattered,' Gayle said. 'The electric power went off, and that would have knocked out your override as well.'

'You have an irritating habit of being right.' He sounded frustated. In the sudden darkness she could see nothing, but she could hear him moving around, and then his hand brushed her face. 'Sorry,' he said. 'I'm just trying to take my coat off so I don't suffocate. Why did they build these things so small?'

'Why bother to take off the coat? It's just a flicker. The power will be back on in a minute.'

'I don't believe in wasting energy. Pardon me for not being a gentleman, but I'm going to sit down.'

'Which floor are we on, anyway?'

'The last time I looked, we were between ten and

eleven. Damn slow lift—a modern one would have had us there before this happened.'

'I thought you liked this old building.'

'Only when it functions properly,' he grumbled. But as the minutes ticked on, counted by the tiny light in his digital watch, and the lift grew warmer, the note of humour came back to Jared's voice. 'Well, perhaps you aren't always right, Miss Bradley. You might as well take off your coat and join me on the floor.'

Too bad for him, she thought, that she wasn't one of the dozens of women who would have jumped at the chance! Gayle hadn't moved since the lights had gone out. Now she sighed. 'This is getting a little tiresome.'

He pulled open the tiny compartment that held the emergency 'phone, and swore. Then the tiny watch light flared, and Gayle could see the raw ends of wires that filled the little box. But there was no 'phone to be seen.

'Maintenance told me they were having trouble with the emergency wiring,' she said drearily. 'I wonder if anyone even knows we're here?'

Jared pushed the wires back into the box and slammed it shut. 'Thomas does.'

'He'll be half an hour getting his thoughts together.' One of the pins that held her hair up in the neat coil at the back of her neck had caught in the wrought iron grillwork. As she pulled away, her hair cascaded down around her face and pins went spinning away on to the carpeted floor. 'Darn it,' she said, 'There went my hair. Will you loan me your watch so I can use the light to look for my pins?'

'No. It's solar powered and I don't know how long it will hold a charge.'

'We could test it,' she said sweetly.

'Sit down, Miss Bradley.'

She tried to put her hair up again, but she could find only two pins, so she soon gave it up as hopeless. 'This must be what it feels like inside a tomb.'

'Don't tell me you have claustrophobia. I don't care a bit whether you do or not—just don't tell me.'

She shifted, trying to find a comfortable position on the floor. 'You have no consideration for your employees' comfort,' she accused. 'You could at least put benches in the lifts.'

'Put a bench in here and you'd have room left for one person. Or possibly two, if they were intimate friends.' The tone of his voice left no room for doubt about his definition.

Gayle bit her lip and kept silent. She'd already strayed into impertinence; she didn't dare keep talking to him like that. The darkness seemed to make her self-imposed rules harder to follow. She must watch out, she warned herself, because when they got out of this lift he'd still be the boss and she the secretary.

'Who was the man who brought you to work this morning?' he asked suddenly.

Gayle stammered a moment. 'A friend of my brother's,' she said finally.

'Steady date?' His tone was casual.

He didn't care, she thought. He was just making casual conversation, amusing himself with his secretary's little flirtations to while away the minutes in the dark. Suddenly irritated, she said, 'He'd like to be.' She sounded defiant, and a little childish.

The comment didn't touch him. 'All weekend would seem steady enough to me,' he said mildly.

'What does that mean?'

'You were certainly out with someone all day yesterday and all of last night. You weren't answering your telephone.'

'I'd unplugged it. Wait a minute—you were trying to call? How did you get the number?'

'Believe it or not, Miss G. L. Bradley, no address given, I can actually read a telephone directory. I've known my alphabet at least since I was twelve.'

'Sorry,' she murmured.

'By the way, what is your name, anyway? Do you ever write it down anywhere, or were you christened with only initials?'

'It's habit, I guess. A woman who lives alone is a fool to put her name on the mailbox. Initials mean that it could be a man living there—it's less dangerous.'

'Golda,' he speculated. 'Gertrude, Gladys, Guinevere——'

Time to put a stop to this, she thought. 'Do I look like a Guinevere? Really.'

'No. But to be scrupulously fair, you don't look like a Gladys either.'

'I suppose I have to be thankful for that.' She sighed. 'It's Gayle.'

He didn't comment. A little later, he said, 'I wonder if anyone is trying to get us out of here.'

Curiosity was prickling deep inside her, and it irritated her. What difference did it make whether he liked her name or hated it? And why should she even want to know what he thought? 'How long have we been here?'

The flicker of the light on his watch hurt her eyes against the total blackness. 'Twenty minutes.'

'It feels like forever.' Gayle put her head back against the wall with a sigh.

'Just don't tell anyone that being stranded in a lift with me was the most boring time of your life,' he pleaded. 'It will ruin my reputation.'

Gayle thought that if word got out of the building's baulky lifts, there would be girls standing in line hoping to get trapped in one with him. But she didn't think his self-esteem needed any boosting, so she didn't say it.

'We'll give it another five minutes, and then we'll start pounding on the door. Somebody should hear us.'

'The way this building is built? The walls are a foot thick. Why were you trying to call me yesterday, anyway?' she asked.

'You did say you'd work this weekend,' he reminded.

'I thought we might get a few things done over the 'phone.'

'Sorry. I really did just have it unplugged.'

'If you say so.' Now he was the one who sounded bored, and half-sleepy. Without the ventilating fan, the elevator was getting warm and stuffy.

Or is it me that he's bored with? she asked herself. That was just as probable. 'How did the trip go? You and Russell Glenn must have come to an agreement, since you're back so early.'

He sighed. 'No. By the time I got there, Russell had attached some interesting new terms to the sale.'

The light flickered on and the ventilating fan wheezed. Jared jumped to his feet and pushed the button for the next floor. 'I'm getting off this thing as soon as possible,' he announced.

Gayle held her breath, but the lift creaked and lurched and jolted into motion. Half a minute later, the door opened on a crowd gathered in the twelfth-floor lobby. Thomas was there, Gayle saw, and a group of workmen in hard hats.

'Nice of you to come to meet us,' Jared told them with icy politeness.

The maintenance supervisor said, 'We were just about to drop a rope down the shaft and try a rescue. I'm glad we didn't have to.'

Gayle shuddered at the thought of being hoisted up that pitch-black shaft. Her hair spilled over her face, reminding her that she didn't look her best at the moment.

'What's the problem, anyway?' Jared demanded. 'And by the way, I want the emergency 'phones back in those lifts before noon!'

He and the maintenance man walked off towards the stairs, their voices fading. Gayle caught a few words—'accident ... main power transformer ... all over downtown ...' but she couldn't hear it all. The crowd of workmen picked up their tools and dispersed, and in moments the lobby was almost empty.

Thomas touched her arm. 'I'm sorry, Miss Bradley.'

'It wasn't your fault, Thomas.'

'But I forgot you were in there. And it looks like you didn't enjoy it a bit.' He sounded truly remorseful.

Gayle started to laugh and pushed her hair back out of her eyes. 'I may look a bit dishevelled at the moment, but it doesn't mean that I was attacked in the lift, Thomas. Mr Logan has better sense than that.'

He looked doubtful. 'If you say so, Miss Bradley.'

'How am I supposed to get to my office?' she asked.

'Oh, the lifts are fine now. Some jerk down the street didn't know how to handle a boom truck and got too close to the electric lines. He almost electrocuted himself, and he knocked the power out for blocks. But now it's fixed.'

Gayle looked at the lift with loathing. 'I suppose I have to ride in it again sometime.'

'It might as well be right now,' Thomas agreed. 'I'll take you up if you like.'

'I think I can handle it.' But she held her breath most of the way up, and only let herself feel relief when she was safe on the eighteenth floor.

She looked into the mirror inside the tiny closet where she hung up her coat, and groaned. Her hair looked as if she hadn't bothered to brush it at all that morning. No wonder Thomas had jumped to the conclusion that Jared Logan had been running his fingers through it!

'And I'm delighted that he wasn't,' she said firmly to her reflection. She was fighting to get it all back into the smooth coil when one of the typists from the secretarial pool brought up the mail. The girl's eyes were malicious. 'We heard you had an exciting half-hour this morning,' she said, putting the stack of envelopes on Gayle's desk. 'Tell me—what's it like to be stuck in an lift with the boss?'

'Nothing to write home about,' Gayle said shortly.

'Looks to me like you had a good time,' the girl speculated.

'Just about as exciting as having a tooth extracted.' Gayle started to open the mail.

'Nothing out of the ordinary?' the girl quizzed, and sat down on the corner of the desk. 'Is it true that he has a couch in his office that pulls out into a bed?'

'No.' Just then her telephone chimed and saved her. She answered it with gratitude.

'Gayle?' Rachel's voice was anxious. 'They told me you were trapped in the lift this morning.'

'News certainly travels fast, doesn't it?' Had everybody in Denver heard about her adventure?

The girl from the secretarial pool gave up and left, a sullen look on her face.

'I just called to see if you and Larry had a good time this weekend——'

'Speaking of Larry, you can tell him I'm not interested.'

'Gayle, what's the matter with you? He's a wonderful, warm, loving——'

'I don't like to be absorbed, Rachel. I need my privacy.'

'It seems to me that privacy is all you've had in the last few years. I'd think you'd be ready for a little human warmth.'

'Well, Larry isn't my choice of bonfire. Thanks, honey, but I'll do my own looking in the future.'

Rachel sighed unhappily. 'I wish you would really do that, Gayle. But you're just hiding from life. You aren't interested in living.'

'Do you mind if we take this conversation up again on Friday night?'

'You're insisting on dying with Craig, inch by inch! If you were his widow, it would be easier to understand. But you never even had an engagement ring!'

'You don't have to wear a ring to love someone.

Look, I really do have work to do. I'll talk to you later, Rachel.' She didn't give her sister-in-law a chance to argue.

Was Rachel right, she wondered as she slowly reduced the mail to piles? Was it foolish of her to spend so much time alone—to prefer solitude to the company of other people? If Craig had lived, she wouldn't have felt that way. But he was dead. Was it so wrong of her not to want to put another man in his place?

I'll think about it later, she told herself firmly. It wasn't professional to think of personal matters in the office.

By the time the maintenance supervisor came out of Jared Logan's office half an hour later, perspiring, Gayle had the mail sorted and had started on her morning's work.

The maintenance man jerked his head towards the closed door of Jared's office. 'He's on a rampage this morning,' he commented.

'Do you blame him?'

'No. But you were stuck in the lift too, and you're not jumping all over me. Besides, it wasn't me who shorted out the power line and got you trapped.'

The intercom on Gayle's desk said, 'Will you come in, Miss Bradley?' The maintenance man was still beside her desk, muttering under his breath, when she left her office.

Jared was staring out over the city skyline, his back towards her, and he didn't seem to hear her come in. She stood there silently for a couple of minutes, and then said softly, 'Mr Logan? Would you like me to come back later?'

He turned then, and came back to the glass table, motioning her to take a chair across from him. Gayle put her notebook down. She was uneasily aware that he didn't take his eyes off her, and it was hard not to fidget under that midnight-blue gaze.

'I want to dictate a few notes about my trip,' he said,

and she picked up her pencil with relief. The words flowed over her and into a stream of perfect shorthand on the notepad. Gayle heard what he was talking about, and she could have read it back easily, but none of it really stayed in her head. It was all ordinary stuff—facts and figures about Softek that he'd picked up while talking to Russell Glenn. Until——

Abruptly, she heard herself interrupting him. 'I'm not certain I heard all of that last sentence correctly.'

'Read it back,' he said. He leaned back in his big leather chair, his fingers laced at the nape of his neck.

She glanced at the notepad and read, '"Then Mr Glenn said he didn't think he was interested in selling Softek after all but would like to merge his entire business operation with Logan Electronics, and suggested that the best way to bring that about was if I married his daughter." Can that be right?'

'You got it—word for word.'

'No wonder you have the jitters this morning.' She couldn't have stopped herself from saying that if there had been a dagger pointed at her heart. And, she had to admit, if there had been one handy, Jared Logan would probably have thrown it at her.

'Do you blame me?' He sounded tired.

She put her pencil down. 'He actually said that?'

'Oh, he didn't come out with it quite that plainly. He told me that a merger sounded like a much better idea than the purchase, and then a few minutes later he said, "You've never met my daughter, have you? She'll inherit the business", and so on.'

'And from that you think that he wants to marry her off? Your reasoning sounds a little strained to me.'

'I beg your pardon, Miss Bradley, but you were not there. I was.'

Gayle was honestly puzzled. 'And from those two statements, you jumped to the conclusion that he was matchmaking? How do you know that's what he meant?'

'Believe me, when a man has been a target as long as I have, he knows when someone is threatening his freedom.'

'For all you know, she's ten years old and still playing with dolls——'

'She's twenty-one and just finishing college.'

Gayle shrugged. This conversation was beginning to sound like farce. 'Cheer up. She might not be any more interested in you than you are in her.'

'She isn't going to get the chance.' He sounded grim.

'That sounds definite,' she murmured. 'Shall I just close the files on Softek, then?'

'No.' He got up from his chair and strode across to the long windows. 'No. I'm not going to give up—I'm going to buy that corporation.'

Gayle was silent for a long moment, then the humour of the situation overwhelmed her. 'You have to give Russell Glenn credit for a new merchandising idea. It's a lot more interesting than giving away green stamps.'

'Not to me.' He sounded bitterly frustrated.

'So what are you going to do, Mr Logan?'

He tossed himself down in the leather chair again. 'What do you recommend, Miss Bradley? It's a difficult situation here. If I offend Russell Glenn, he won't sell me what I want at any price. But if I don't get myself out of this coil somehow, I'll find myself married to what's-her-name without even having to propose.'

'I still say she might have different ideas——'

'I appreciate your efforts to keep me humble, Miss Bradley, but let me assure you that I am a very eligible bachelor.'

'I think you have a problem,' Gayle said cheerfully. And I'm going to enjoy watching you get out of this pickle, she thought.

'Just what do you think I should do? Any brilliant suggestions?'

'Not a one.' Gayle forced herself to sound calm. 'Things like this don't happen in real life, Mr Logan—

fathers don't include their daughters in merger plans, for heaven's sake. It's medieval!'

'Oh, I'm sure she knows all about it. In fact,' he mused, 'the whole thing was probably her idea.'

'So what are you going to do?'

'I've already done it. I told Russell Glenn that I would be delighted to meet his daughter, and I invited him to bring her to Denver next weekend to stay at Pino Reposo.'

'But you said——'

He didn't give her a chance to finish. 'Where my fiancée and I would be most happy to entertain them.'

There was dead silence in the room for a full minute. Then Gayle took a deep breath, and held her voice steady with an effort. 'Congratulations,' she said. 'I understand now why you were so upset at the idea of marrying Miss Glenn.'

'Don't be dense,' he said brusquely. 'I have no intention of getting married. I am merely going to convince Russell Glenn that I'm not and never will be free to marry his daughter. Then, just as soon as the papers are signed—Poof! No more engagement.'

'I see.' Gayle doodled a design on the page of her notebook. 'Who's the lucky lady? And are you going to tell her that she's only temporary? Natalie Weston would be delighted, I'm sure, and as an actress of sorts she'd be perfect for the part . . .'

'Natalie is married. She'd hardly be convincing to Russ Glenn as my fiancée.'

'Goodness, how could that have slipped my mind?' But her voice was beginning to sound a little brittle, as if the whole situation was edging out of her control. Why, she wondered, was he telling her all of this? 'Then—who?' she asked, just a little fearfully.

He started to smile, like one of the zoo lions who has just enjoyed a good meal, and said, 'Russell Glenn is very anxious to meet you, Gayle.'

Her hands clenched convulsively on her pencil.

'I told him you'd be delighted to entertain him at Pino Repsos this weekend,' he said silkily. 'Won't you, darling?'

CHAPTER THREE

'Is this some sort of——' Her voice cracked, and she had to clear her throat and start over. 'If this is your idea of a joke . . .'

Jared didn't comment. He was watching her, she thought, with considerable interest.

'I'm sorry I laughed at you,' she said, trying to keep her voice steady. 'I quite understand that you don't find the situation funny.'

'Oh, I'm beginning to see traces of humour in it,' he admitted.

'There's bound to be a solution. Perhaps if you——'

'I've found the only solution, Gayle,' he said quietly.

She swallowed hard, and then said, 'No,' on a note of gentle defiance.

He raised an eyebrow. 'The one thing I never expected,' he mused, 'was that I would finally bring myself to propose to a lady, only to be rejected.'

'This isn't a proposal, it's a—three-ring circus,' Gayle snapped. 'And I won't do it.'

'Do you like your job here?' he asked gently.

'I used to!'

'Well, if you'd like to keep it——' The rest of the sentence hung in the air. It didn't have to be spoken.

Gayle felt as if the room was spinning.

'I'm sorry if your boyfriend doesn't appreciate your new assignment. To be honest, I hadn't even considered that you might be dating someone.'

Good old reliable Miss Bradley, she thought bitterly—always there to cover for the boss. Of course he hadn't considered that she might have a man in her life. He probably thought that no one could possibly be interested in Gayle. Anger at his assumption made her say, 'Well, I am dating. And I'm not interested in putting him on hold just because you got yourself into a spot, Mr Logan.'

He looked her over from head to toe, and Gayle thought that she might as well have been a piece of merchandise, for all he cared. Then he asked mildly, 'Are you sleeping with him?'

She was furious. 'I wasn't aware that my morals had anything to do with my job!'

'Well, as long as you're discreet, I can't see that it matters what you do. I promise to return you to him unharmed, just as soon as Russell Glenn and I have signed the sale contracts.'

Actually, she had to admit, there would be one advantage to this little play. If she was pretending to be engaged, Larry would darn well have to leave her alone.

'It's only for a few days, anyway,' he said impatiently. 'Russell and Krystal——'

'I thought you couldn't remember her name.'

'I've spent all weekend trying to forget it.'

'Did you get to meet this girl?'

'No. She just graduated from college last month and is off on a trip—a reward from Daddy. She'll be back this week. They'll arrive on Friday and leave Monday morning. After that Russell will be in California and you and I can do as we darn well please. We'll have to keep up the fiction if he happens to call, of course, but once the weekend is over——'

She shook her head. 'I still don't like it. I appreciate the honour and all that, but I wasn't cut out to be an actress. You'll have to find someone else.'

'Just why do you think I chose you, anyway?' His tone was brutal.

Gayle reflected on all the women she had watched pass through his life in the last two years. There had never been one who was less than lovely. They were all tall, slim, elegant, dressed in the latest and most expensive fashion. Their jewelry was never fake and their fingernails always were. 'I ought to have known it wasn't my charm,' she said with a bitter note. 'All right, tell me—why did you pick me? Any one of the women you've dated would be thrilled to pretend to be your fiancée——'

'And any one of them would promptly forget that she is only pretending. I have no intention of putting my head in a noose.'

'Charming attitude you have about marriage,' she muttered.

'I don't believe in marriage. I have never met a woman that I could stand to look at over the breakfast table for the rest of my life——'

'There's an easy solution to that,' Gayle interrupted. 'Take her breakfast in bed every morning.'

He ignored the interruption. 'You're elected, my dear. You might as well make the best of it.'

Gayle shook her head. 'Not me, I'm sure you'll find someone who is interested in your proposition.'

'It has to be you, Gayle. I told Russell Glenn a very charming story about how I tumbled into love with my secretary.'

'That figures,' she said bitterly. 'You could charm a rattlesnake.'

'Considering that he took me by surprise, it was a wonderful story. Cheer up, Gayle. It's not exactly a fate worse than death.'

She was silent. Somewhere at the back of her mind, panic fluttered, and she tried to drown it. He was right, after all. A few days of pretending to be the future Mrs Jared Logan wouldn't change anything.

'It won't last long,' he said again. 'I wouldn't be surprised if he cuts a deal next weekend at Pino Reposo, as soon as he sees that his other idea is out of the question.'

'I wouldn't hold my breath,' Gayle muttered. He had stopped asking if she would do it, she noticed, and gone on to arranging the details. That was typical of Jared

Logan, and she supposed there was no point in arguing with him. He's made up his mind. And he was absolutely serious about firing her if she refused this request.

Request, heck, she thought inelegantly. This is a spot of blackmail.

'Of course, I'll pay you for the extra time you'll have to devote,' he said.

Gayle saw the look that he flicked toward her high-necked black dress and braced herself for the next remark.

'If you could arrange to wear something besides black all the time, it would help the image.' He rubbed a thoughtful hand along his jaw. 'Why don't you take the afternoon off and go buy some clothes? Charge them to me—consider it a bonus.'

She could just see herself in one of the exclusive boutiques on Larimer Square, charging a wardrobe to Jared Logan. They'd laugh her out of the shop. Or, even worse, they'll sell her the clothes, and assume that she was his mistress . . . 'No thanks,' she said stiffly. 'I don't take gifts of clothing from any man, Mr Logan.'

'Oh, it isn't a gift,' he said, sounding a little surprised at her reaction. 'Consider it a bribe.'

'I'm amazed,' she said, and ice tinkled in her voice, 'that you think Russell Glenn will actually be convinced that you could fall for me. I suppose I should be flattered, but I must admit that gratitude escapes me at the moment.'

'I must admit to a few questions about that myself,' he said mildly. 'He's going to take some convincing. But you were the only port in the storm, so to speak. I had to do something while he was still just tossing hints, before he came out with the suggestion in plain English. You were the only possibility that came to mind. Frankly, I didn't think you'd mind.'

Gayle's temper flared. 'You expected me to be pleased at the idea of being engaged to you?' She shuddered, delicately. 'Now that we understand each other . . .' she added sweetly.

'Just remember this,' he pointed out. 'The result is up to you. The quicker you can convince Russell Glenn that we're so deeply in love that his precious daughter doesn't stand a chance, the quicker he'll sell me his computer division. Then we'll be through with this mad game, and you can go back to your boyfriend.'

She'd forgotten about Larry entirely, but she was darned if she'd admit that to him. 'Believe me, Mr Logan,' she said tartly, 'you can't be any more anxious than I am to have this mess over and done with.'

I can't believe what I got myself into this time, she moaned as she locked herself into the women's lounge. She stared at her white face in the mirror and began rhythmically splashing cold water on her cheeks, hoping to wake herself up from this nightmare. But there was no escaping reality, and so she dried her face and went back to her desk. Perhaps hard work would make it go away.

Jared had gone out to the factory, which sprawled in a brand new building on the outskirts of Denver. She should have been able to breathe a little easier because he was gone. Instead she found herself jumping three feet every time her door opened, because it might be him back again.

The advertising manager came in late in the afternoon. Gayle sat up straight when the door opened, and then relaxed. Another half-hour, she was thinking. If he doesn't come back in the next half-hour, I can go home. He didn't ask me to stay late tonight, so he can't be surprised if I leave right on time . . . If I can just have some time to think about this, perhaps I can get my mind straightened out again.

'Is J. L. in?' the ad man asked. He was a big, breezy-mannered man who favoured loud plaid sports jackets.

Today it was emerald and orange, with green trousers. The combination hurt Gayle's eyes.

'He went out to the factory, Ron.' She made the last two editing changes in her letter, and keyed in the command that told the computer to type it. The printer rolled up a sheet of paper and started to clatter.

Ron perched on the corner of her desk, and Gayle, trying to look casual, pushed her chair back.

He grinned. 'While the cat's away, sweetheart— Though it isn't kind to compare you to a mouse, is it? And it's also not accurate.'

'Ron, did you come in for business or to feed me compliments in the fond hope that someday I might take you seriously?'

He sighed. 'Business, actually, I wondered if J. L. was finished with the ad campaign. But since he's not here, I might as well——'

Gayle handed him the portfolio. 'Next time, I'd leave out the funny pictures,' she recommended. 'Unless of course you like taking chances with your job. Natalie Weston is not a good subject to poke fun at just now.'

Ron shrugged. 'I'm not worried. I doubt Natalie is the girl to make our J. L. lose his sense of humour. Now I kind of liked that picture.' He started to rummage through the stack.

'Mr Logan took it out. And he didn't look pleased.'

Ron mused, 'I wonder if he added it to his collection of the beauties who have spent the night in his bed. Quite a little black book he must have by now— illustrations and all.'

Gayle started to colour despite herself. She turned away to pick up her letter, but Ron had seen her expression.

He leered at her, just a little. 'It's probably gone into the third volume by now. He ought to offer excerpts to the men's magazines. Tell me, Gayle, what is it with him? Why do the women fall all over him like that?'

She could see honest puzzlement in his eyes. 'I don't

know, Ron,' she evaded. 'I'm sure the money doesn't hurt.'

'Yes, it must be nice to have an old man who owns a string of banks,' he remarked. 'But I don't think that's it. If Jared Logan was only a stockroom clerk, there would be girls standing in line waiting for him.'

He was right. I'm just fortunate, Gayle thought, that I'm immune to Jared Logan's brand of charm. Another thing to be grateful to Craig for, she told herself.

'You don't go for him, do you?' Ron asked, and she wondered uneasily if he could read her mind. 'J. L.'s magic doesn't work on you. So what are you looking for, Gayle? Or have you found it?'

All I want is peaceful serenity, she thought. Instead, here I am caught up in this ridiculous charade—pretending to be in love with Jared Logan. And all I was doing was minding my own business.

The telephone chimed, and she answered it, glad that it had interrupted Ron's question. There was no easy way to tell him that what she was looking for wasn't him, any more than it was Larry. Or Jared Logan, come to that. Why did everyone seem to feel that a woman couldn't be happy without a man?

'Miss Bradley?'

The voice was crisp, pleasant, brisk. Gayle fumbled in her memory for one brief second, and then relaxed. 'Hello, Mrs Logan.'

Elizabeth Logan laughed. 'No wonder my beloved brother-in-law swears by you. You are a jewel. I called to thank you for the lovely crystal vase Jared sent for my birthday.'

'Mr Logan isn't here at the moment,' Gayle began.

'No, dear, you misunderstand. I didn't call to talk to Jared. I'll tell him how beautiful the vase is next time I see him. But I know quite well that he doesn't know Steuben from Lalique, so it didn't take much intuition to know who chose it. Thank you, Miss Bradley.'

Warmth spread all over Gayle. She'd never met

Elizabeth Logan; Jared's brother and his wife were as busy with their careers in Chicago as Jared himself was in Denver. But from the little she knew of the woman, gleaned from telephone conversations and his comments, she had been impressed by Elizabeth's whiplash intelligence. And her manners, Gayle thought now, which certainly put to shame those of the western branch of the Logan family . . .

Elizabeth was talking comfortably on when Natalie Weston came into the office on a wave of expensive perfume. She looked around, bestowed a vague smile on Ron, and stood in front of the desk, tapping her foot impatiently on the plush carpet and staring pointedly at Gayle.

Gayle finally cupped her hand over the mouthpiece and said, 'May I help you, Mrs Weston?'

'Unless you'd rather keep gossiping on the 'phone,' Natalie said with arched eyebrows. 'I'm certain Mr Logan would like to hear about this conduct from his so-called perfect secretary. Is he in?'

'No. He didn't say when he would be back.'

'I'll wait,' Natalie said flatly. She sat down, crossed one slim, elegant leg over the other, and impatiently rotated her ankle, admiring the effect of the small foot in its impossibly high-heeled shoe.

Elizabeth said, into Gayle's ear, 'Are you there, Miss Bradley?'

'Of course, Mrs Logan,' she said. 'I'll tell him you called . . .'

'Mrs Logan!' Natalie Weston sounded horrified. Her foot stopped moving.

Ron laughed derisively. 'Why are you so surprised that there is a Mrs Logan? After all, there's a Mr Weston somewhere, and that doesn't seem to stand in your way.'

'Why don't you mind your own business?' Natalie said crossly.

'You apparently weren't invited to come here,' Ron

speculated, 'or you'd have known that J. L. isn't here. I'd advise that you take yourself off. Our J. L. is a man who likes to issue his own invitations, and he doesn't like to find ladies lying in wait for him in unexpected places.'

Natalie fixed him with a glare that should have turned him into cinders where he stood. But Ron just smiled and said, 'I'd bet a hundred dollars right now that J. L.'s plans for the evening are already made. And I'd add another hundred that says you're not included in them, Nat.'

A cool, amused voice from the doorway answered. None of them had heard him come in, and three heads turned toward him as Jared Logan said, 'That's right, Ron. You win your bet. And now if you two would take yourselves out of here, my fiancée and I are going to the jewellers' to buy an engagement ring. Are you ready, Gayle?'

I think I'm going to be sick, Gayle thought drearily. She closed her eyes so the room wouldn't revolve quite so fast, and when she experimentally opened them again, Natalie and Ron had vanished.

'Is that telephone call for me?' Jared asked.

She sighed and relinquished the 'phone with relief. 'It's your sister-in-law.'

He frowned as he took it. Then he shrugged philosophically, perched on the corner of the desk, and said, 'Hello, Elizabeth. Sorry about the wait, but you can certainly afford to be left on hold.'

Gayle tuned the conversation out. She could still see the horror in Natalie Weston's face and the way her lovely features had drawn up into a fierce mask. It would have been funny, if it had been anyone but herself who was the cause of that look. And then there had been Ron, but his expression had been more comical than anything else, as he left.

It was all so unnecessary, she fumed. What could

have tempted Jared Logan to make such a scene? And
for what, she wondered. All she was supposed to do
was be charming for three days of entertaining the
Glenns. There had been no need to bring the whole
world in on it.

He was laughing now, obviously unconcerned about
the havoc he had just created. By the time he put the
'phone down, Gayle had herself under control.

'Why did you do that?' she asked calmly.

'What? Talk to Elizabeth? Because she called. She'd
have been very suspicious if I hadn't.'

'You know what I mean. Why did you tell Ron and
Mrs Weston that we are—you know——' she stumbled
over the word.

'Engaged? Call it an irresistible impulse. I always
wanted to see what would happen if I said that.'

She could have thrown the unabridged dictionary at
him. 'You realise that it will be all over the building by
tomorrow morning?'

'Oh, quite. As a matter of fact, I'd be surprised if it
takes that long.' He sounded quite cheerful about it, she
thought.

'Don't you mind?'

'Why should I? It is a fact, you know, even if it isn't
quite the complete story.'

'I didn't expect that this would be announced. I can't
imagine what you're thinking of!'

He shook his head sadly. 'The first rule of business,
Gayle, is that you never try to keep a secret that is
bound to slip out anyway. It always leaks, and then it
looks as if you're out of control.'

'I am out of control!' she said. Her voice was
trembling with rage.

'I know,' he said kindly. 'You'll get over it, once the
newness wears off. Besides, when you make a
straightforward public announcement, it never occurs to
anyone to wonder if you might be hiding something
behind it. Result, in this case—everyone will be too

preoccupied with the seven days' wonder of our engagement to wonder what we're really up to.'

'I'm glad you believe that. Why not just keep it quiet? No one even needs to know, and then when it is all over——'

He was shaking his head. 'But it can't be hidden. The news will get out that you spent the weekend with me at Pino Reposo. What do you think the employees would have to say about that?'

That I'm just another of a long series, she was thinking.

He answered his own question. 'They'd know there was something fishy. If it was just an affair, I'd take you to the love nest—but not Pino Reposo.'

'So you *do* know what they call the penthouse,' she said.

'Of course. Not a very original name, is it? A bunch of creative people like these. I'd think they could come up with something catchier than that,' he mused. Then, as if he'd remembered the original topic: 'To say nothing about the ring. Someone will be bound to see you wearing it, and——'

'I will not wear a diamond ring.' Her voice was flat. 'I absolutely refuse.'

Jared sighed. 'You never used to be this much trouble; do you realise that? Is Russell Glenn going to believe that a man in my position can't afford to buy his future wife a ring?'

'I don't care what Russell Glenn thinks!'

'But you do want him to believe that we're engaged, so I can buy Softek, so we can break this off soon, so you can be free——' He let that sink in a minute, and then stood up. 'Where will I find your coat? The jeweller is supposed to stay late for us, but I can't promise that he won't get tired of waiting and go on home.'

'I couldn't be so lucky,' Gayle said bitterly.

She kept silent for the next ten minutes, while Jared

cajoled her into her coat, down the lift, and out to the parking ramp where he tucked her solicitously into the front seat of a dark blue Jaguar. She bit her tongue to keep from telling him how pretty it was, but he saw her hand caress the supple leather.

As he slid into the driver's seat, she saw that he was smiling. 'It is a pretty car, isn't it?' he said, and answered his own question. 'Oh, yes, it's lovely, Jared. Why, thank you, Gayle, I'm so glad you like it.'

'Mr Logan . . .' she said frostily. 'I've changed my mind. Let's go back to the office and I'll draw up my resignation letter. It will save you the effort of firing me, and——'

The Jag's engine roared. 'Too late,' he said comfortably. 'I'd have to sue you for breach of promise if you backed out at this point.'

'Is there still such a thing?' she asked, momentarily diverted.

He turned toward her, his smile flashing. 'I haven't the faintest idea. But it would be an affair of honour. Shall we say, attorneys at twenty paces?'

'Mr Logan, I really think——'

'Miss Bradley,' he mocked, 'I think you'd better stop calling me Mr Logan, if you know what's good for you. The jeweller is a friend of mine, by the way. And I've told him what an unusual sense of humour you have, so he isn't going to take you seriously when you protest that you're being forced into this.'

'Mr——' She saw his eyes flash, and swallowed the word. 'All right. Jared.' It felt strange—almost ticklish—on her tongue. 'I think we'd better reconsider.'

'Reconsider what?' he demanded. 'I'm only asking for your help. It's part of your job, after all.'

'To pretend to be engaged?' Her voice was rising.

'If I was on my way to Tokyo for a business conference, you wouldn't hesitate to catch a plane with me,' he pointed out.

'That's different!'

'Yes. It would require you to find someone to babysit the dog.'

'I don't have a dog.'

'Good. Then you don't have to worry about him. Here we are.'

How did I get myself into this, she thought wearily. He's finally gone crazy, as all computer people do, sooner or later . . .

He came around the car and held out a hand to help her out. 'This is insane,' she said.

This time there was no humour in his eyes. 'Miss Bradley,' he said firmly. 'If I was forcing you into an actual marriage, here, you would have a legitimate complaint. As it is, I haven't even laid a hand on you . . .'

Gayle looked pointedly down at her gloved hand, locked in his.

He sighed and let go. 'Figuratively speaking,' he said. 'Let's be reasonable. You're as safe as a tomb with me. So stop screaming as if you were about to be raped.'

She bit her lip hard. Finally, with a minimum of control regained, she said, 'I must sound silly, thinking that I am in any danger from you.'

'Well, yes, you do,' he said. He sounded genuinely sorry. 'You're a very nice girl, Gayle, but just——'

'Not your type.' Now she was icily furious. He would pay for this if it was the last thing she ever accomplished, she resolved. He was telling the truth, she knew, and she was glad that she wasn't his type. But to do it in such a cold-blooded, brutal way——

'That's it,' he said, sounding delighted that she understood. He pushed open the door of one of Denver's most exclusive jewellery stores, and let her precede him.

'Mr Logan!' A little man in a dark business suit hurried towards them. 'And the future Mrs Logan. Welcome. Let me take your coats. And come straight into my office. I have some rings ready to show you—

and then of course some lovely diamonds, so we can design a special setting if you like——'

'Not diamonds,' Jared said firmly. 'Gayle has just told me that she refuses to wear a diamond engagement ring.'

'That wasn't quite what I said,' Gayle muttered.

He gave her a loving smile, took her coat, held her chair. 'And I must agree. An engagement like this one should not be symbolised by an ordinary diamond.'

The jeweller pushed up his glasses and looked at Gayle through the magnifying lenses, as if she were a very flawed gem. 'What kind of stone did you have in mind?' he asked her.

Jared said, thoughtfully, 'Something unusual.'

'There's ruby, of course, or emerald.'

'Too ordinary,' Jared said grandly.

'Or alexandrite. Or precious topaz . . .'

'Come now,' Jared scolded. 'This is an engagement ring, not a birthstone.'

'Pearls or opals—but they're too soft a stone to be lasting,' the man fretted.

'Oh, by all means this has to wear well,' Gayle said, and didn't care that the raw edge of sarcasm sliced through her words.

'What colour did you have in mind?' the jeweller asked her.

Gayle thought for a moment, and raised her head defiantly. 'Orange,' she said. There! That ought to fix Jared Logan, she thought.

He just smiled. 'What a brilliant idea. It will be stunning with your brown hair and eyes,' he said. 'Perhaps, after we get the ring, we should look for a dress in the same colour. Just a little something to wear this weekend—to increase the impact of the announcement, you might say.'

So much for that effort to disconcert him, she thought.

The furrows disappeared from the jeweller's forehead.

'I have it!' he said. 'The very thing. It's in the safe—a five-carat padparadschah, surrounded by tapered baguettes, channel set in platinum . . .' He hurried off, humming under his breath.

'Would you like to translate that?' Gayle asked.

'Oh, he was still speaking English. At least, I think he was,' Jared muttered.

The little man came bustling back, a velvet box in his hand.

'I haven't the vaguest idea what you're talking about,' Gayle told him.

'Ah.' He smiled. 'Of course you don't. The padparadschah is the most rare of the sapphire family.'

'It's blue? But I said——'

'Oh, no. Sapphires come in violet, yellow, green—every colour of the mineral corundum except red.' He gave her a self-satisfied smile. 'Do you know why there are no red sapphires?'

'I haven't a clue.'

'Because red corundum is known as ruby,' he said, delighted to be able to instruct her. 'The padparadschah is—well, I suppose you could call it burnt orange in colour. The word means Lotus Flower.'

'And the rest of that description? What does it mean?' Jared asked. He leaned forward to get a look at the velvet box, but the jeweller moved it away. 'In a moment, Mr Logan. The sapphire family is associated with the planet Venus, named of course for the god of love. A most apt choice for an engagement ring.' He gave Gayle an appraising look, as if she was a student he was especially proud of. 'And now——' He opened the velvet box and turned it slowly toward them under the brilliant lights.

Gayle drew in a long, painful, astonished breath. In the centre of the ring winked an enormous pinkish-orange stone, flashing fire. Around it, pulling the eye toward the centre, lay a dozen baguette diamonds, like rays shining from the central light source.

'If you'll notice,' the jeweller said, 'the baguettes are cut at an angle—tapered to emphasise the centre stone. And instead of being held by prongs, they're set in a channel here formed by the platinum base.'

Jared was lounging in his chair. 'Like it, hmm?' he murmured.

'It's all right,' Gayle said calmly, but she knew that her first long look at the ring had told him everything he needed to know.

'We'll take it.'

The jeweller glanced at the tag on the ring. 'It's——'

Jared hushed him with a wave of the hand. 'Send me the bill,' he said. 'Don't you remember that the bride is never supposed to know how much her ring costs?'

The man didn't argue. 'Let's get your ring size,' he told Gayle. He bustled off again to get the necessary equipment.

She picked up the box and watched as the padparadschah fractured the light and sent it back to her eyes in rays of orange, gold, yellow, green.

'Fell in love with it, didn't you?' Jared said lazily.

'It's a beautiful ring.' She kept her voice just as steady as his.

'If you finish this job,' he said, 'and convince Russell Glenn, you can keep the pod-whatever-it is.'

'More bribery?'

'No. Just my grateful gift for your assistance.'

She put the box down and turned to look at him curiously. 'You really want this purchase to go through, don't you?'

'Go to the head of the class,' he mocked. 'I want that computer division so badly I would do anything to get it.'

'Don't you mean, almost anything?' she asked pleasantly. But her heart was cold as she looked into the depths of the fiery ring. Just how far, she wondered, would he go?

CHAPTER FOUR

GAYLE folded a sweater into her suitcase and glanced at her wristwatch, then at the pile of clothes still waiting to be packed. She was feeling harried. In fifteen minutes Jared Logan would be knocking on her door, ready to take her down to Pino Reposo for the weekend, and she had scarcely begun to pack. And, she admitted, that wasn't the only reason she was tense. If she had already packed every item of clothing in her whole wardrobe, she still wouldn't have been prepared for the ordeal that faced her.

The gleaming ring on her left hand caught the light and splintered it, and she stopped for a moment to stare at it, turning her hand slowly back and forth to watch the padparadschah at play. It was a lovely thing. She felt a little guilty about wearing it right now; after all, there was no one around that she needed to impress. But the ring was probably safer on her finger than anywhere else she could put it, and she didn't dare forget to take it with her.

'Tell the truth, Gayle,' she ordered herself. She could no more take the gorgeous thing off than she could stop breathing. How generous it had been of Jared, to tell her that she could keep it once the job was done. It would make a beautiful dinner ring, a piece of art to treasure forever.

But—Generous, my eye, she thought rebelliously. He simply didn't care what this project cost, and the padparadschah ring was just one more investment in the cause—to buy Softek.

It would be a good addition to Jared's little empire. She'd read the management reports, too. Softek was a good, strong firm, specialising in software that was tailored to Logan computers. Without such instruction programs, a computer was no more than a large electronic paperweight; it had no intelligence of its own. With the specialised software that Softek produced, a Logan computer could do almost anything.

Jared had made up his mind, and once that decision had been made, Gayle wouldn't care to have bet against him. But, she wondered, would it be worth the price it would cost him?

She folded another sweater—a new one in a creamy shade of yellow—and thought about Jared Logan. In two years, she had come to know the hard-headed businessman well. He was a man obsessed by a dream, she thought—to make his product not just the best available, but the perfect machine.

'And he's just like one of his darned computers, too,' she scolded. No humanity, no appreciation of the arts or even of beauty. Oh, he liked his creature comforts, she'd grant that—his well-tailored clothes, his luxurious car, his women . . .

Ah, yes, the women. She bit her lip and kept packing as she thought about his women. Gayle didn't doubt that he enjoyed them in much the same way he liked expensive Scotch and the occasional cigar. He sent flowers the next morning not out of appreciation, but because it was expected of him, and the women were contented with that, because they knew and expected nothing else.

They were all just a bit like his computers, she reflected. Push a button on any one of them, and the result was predictable. Different faces, but not a heart anywhere among the whole crowd. Which must be perfectly all right with Jared Logan, she told herself, because he didn't have a heart either.

'Which brings you a long way from wondering why he wants to buy Softek from Russell Glenn,' she muttered, and started to throw clothes into the suitcase at random, trying to hurry. He hated to wait, and she'd much rather not have him angry at her today.

The doorbell and the telephone rang at almost the same instant. She picked up the 'phone, said, 'Hold on a minute, please,' and dropped it into a cushioned chair. The doorbell pealed again. Of all the days for Jared to get impatient, she thought, it has to be today.

Then stubbornness started to rise in her. He could just be that way, she thought. It was his fault she was running behind schedule, anyway; he was the one who had abruptly decided to drive down early, in time for lunch at Pino Reposo. As far as I'm concerned, Gayle thought, he can just sit here and cool his heels. If he argues about it, I can always tell him I've decided not to go. If nothing else, the fireworks would be entertaining.

He didn't look impatient. 'I'm on the 'phone,' she told him as she pulled the door open.

'That's all right. I'll just stand here and quietly starve to death.' His tone was flippant, but his eyes were sombre as he looked her over from head to toe. 'I thought I asked you to expand your wardrobe to include something besides black,' he said.

'I didn't have time to change,' she countered. 'Remember? I'd planned to take the afternoon off to pack, and then you decide we should leave this morning instead.' She didn't give him a chance to answer before she picked up the 'phone.

It was Larry. Why didn't I just ignore the darn thing, she asked herself morosely.

'Rachel said you're off for the weekend.' He sounded sad.

'That's right.' She hadn't told him about the fake engagement. It would take days to explain it all to Larry's satisfaction—probably longer than the engagement would last.

'I was looking forward to some time with you—dinner, maybe, or——'

'Sorry.' Out of the corner of her eye, she watched Jared as he wandered around the room. He paused in front of the Dali print, and she frowned. If I have to explain it to one more man this week, she thought, I'll just break down and cry—and then move it into my bedroom where I'll never have to show it to another male again!

'Gayle?' Larry's voice was plaintive. 'Does it take you that long to decide?'

What had he asked, while she had been woolgathering? 'Perhaps we'd better talk about it next week, Larry. See you then,' she said quickly, and put the 'phone down on his protest.

'It sounds as if the boyfriend isn't too pleased,' Jared observed.

'Would you be?' Gayle asked tartly. 'Think about it. Your girl suddenly turns up engaged to someone else—would you be delighted?'

He looked thoughtful. 'I can't imagine getting myself into that spot. But I suppose I'd just go beat the tar out of the guy.'

'Fortunate for you that Larry isn't that type.' And for her as well; she had enough trouble without adding Larry to her collection.

'Nice etching,' he said, gesturing to the Dali print.

And that's all the threat of Larry means to you, she thought. It just might do Jared Logan good to run into a jealous husband someday. Gayle fervently hoped that she was around to watch the sport.

'Do you like surrealistic stuff?' He sounded a little surprised.

'Why? What did you expect to find on my walls, puppies and kittens cut from old calendars?' She knew her voice was tart, and she didn't care. 'I'm going to finish packing. There's coffee in the kitchen if you want some.'

It took her another half-hour, and by that time Gayle
was ready to scream. Normally she could pack for a
weekend in fifteen minutes, but this time was a puzzler.
Should she take sports clothes? Dinner clothes?

She called down the hall, 'Do you dress for dinner at
Pino Reposo?'

Jared appeared around the corner. 'Normally, yes.
Peters gets a little upset with me if I come to the dining
room without clothes.'

'That wasn't what I meant.' She retreated to the
bedroom, decided that what was already packed would
have to do, and started to close the bag.

He had followed her. 'Though it is an interesting
idea. It gives a whole new outlook on the phrase,
"Don't dress." Let me do that.'

'I'm quite capable.'

He ignored her and zipped the suitcase. 'You amaze
me, Gayle,' he said, glancing around. 'I really expected
that you'd live in a spare room at the convent or
something.'

'Has anyone ever told you that you have no tact?'
She wished that he hadn't come back to the bedroom. The room seemed suddenly very small with him
there.

'Frequently,' he said cheerfully. His eyes fell on the
gold-framed photograph of Craig on her bedside table.
'Boyfriend?'

'Yes.' It wasn't a lie, she told herself. Craig had been
her boyfriend. And, anyway, why should she volunteer
any information to Jared?

'Is it so difficult to remember what he looks like?'

Gayle swallowed hard and maintained an icy silence
while she got her coat and locked the apartment door
behind them.

The Jaguar was at the kerb. Jared settled her luggage
into the back. 'It seems I said something I shouldn't,' he
murmured. 'Sorry. It doesn't matter to me if you're
sleeping with him.'

'I am not——' she snapped, and then bit the words off.

'Really?' He sounded fascinated.

'There are people who are interested in more than sex, Jared. You just don't think there is such a thing as love,' she challenged.

'Yes, I do. I've seen strong men turned into jelly because of it. Take my brother Grady, for instance. The moment Elizabeth gets out of his sight, he fidgets. I think it's cute, actually. I just don't plan to ever let it happen to me.' He smiled down at her, winningly. 'I knew that under the practical exterior you'd turn out to be a hopeless romantic. Now do you understand why I immediately thought of you when I needed a fiancée?'

She wanted to wrench off a piece of the car and hit him with it. 'Of course,' she said sweetly. 'It's because I'm absolutely no threat to your peace of mind.'

He frowned. 'That wasn't what I meant, actually. You're really quite attractive, if you'd only quit wearing black. I just meant that you're no more interested in me than I am in—Sorry.'

She didn't let him back out of it. 'Familiarity breeds contempt?' she said. Her voice was brittle.

'I do seem to be getting myself in deeper and deeper, don't I? At any rate, there's always the boyfriend to keep me in line.'

'That's right,' Gayle murmured. 'Well, Mr Logan, content yourself with this. No matter what you do, you'll be perfectly safe with me.'

He heaved an elaborate sigh. 'You relieve my mind, Miss Bradley.'

He was so comical about it that she had to laugh, and then he set himself to be charming, and she forgot that she had made up her mind not to be charmed.

She'd never been to Pino Reposo. No one at Logan Electronics had, that she knew of. He referred to it

sometimes as his hideaway, the one place where the
world didn't intrude. She had the telephone number,
because she occasionally had to call Peters with a
message. But she had never dared to bother Jared there,
and she was frankly amazed that he would invite Russ
and Krystal Glenn to stay at Pino Reposo. Surely it
would have been easier to reserve a suite at one of the
downtown hotels ...

'What is Peters like?' she asked finally. 'Is he as prim
and proper as he sounds over the 'phone?'

'Oh, yes. He's so nervous about meeting you that he's
afraid he's going to spill the soup all over you at lunch,'
Jared said. He didn't sound terribly interested.

The Jag swept through the streets of a little town and
out into the countryside again. They were climbing
now, and the engine pulled a little harder.

The Rockies must be right in his back yard, Gayle
was thinking. 'Didn't you tell him that it's only a joke?'
she asked.

'Of course not.' He shot a surprised look at her.
'That's the second rule of business, Gayle. You never let
anyone in on a secret who doesn't need to know it.'

'By the time we're through with this production, I'll
have acquired a priceless education,' Gayle mused.

'That's right. I only hope you appreciate it. You
could get a job as a junior executive in any of the
Fortune Five-Hundred companies.'

She was shaking her head. 'Not me. I wouldn't want
to be the boss; I like leaving the headaches to you.'

'Gee, thanks.' He thought about it for a moment. 'I
would miss having you around the office,' he admitted
handsomely. 'You're the best secretary I've ever had.'

'I know. You might remember that before you drag
me into any more silly schemes.'

He just smiled. The Jag slowed, made a sharp turn
through wrought iron gates, and purred up a long drive
bordered by huge pine trees. At the end of the drive was
a sprawling Spanish-style house, its bright tile roof

peeking out from the snow cover. It looked like a Christmas card.

Of course, she thought. Pino Reposo. Pine Rest. But this is his country hideaway? It looks more like a mansion to me.

He parked the Jaguar by the arches that lined the front of the house, and in the sudden silence after the motor died Gayle heard herself say, 'I can't do it.'

He smiled. 'Relax,' he said. 'Peters is even more scared of you than you are of him.'

'That wasn't——' But the moment for protesting was past. He came around the car, helped her out, reached for her luggage.

The front door swung open, and out tumbled a tiny, furry body, barking furiously. It looked like a mechanical toy, and it moved so fast that to Gayle's astounded eyes it was nothing more than a blur. 'I didn't know gerbils barked,' she muttered.

It took Jared three tries to corral the hysterical animal, and then when he scooped the furry body up in one hand, the dog's tiny legs continued to churn the air. Jared looked up with a crooked smile. 'This is not a gerbil,' he said sternly. 'It is a Yorkshire terrier named Underdog.' The dog squirmed in his hand, trying to lick Jared's fingers.

'I can see why he got the name,' Gayle said gravely.

'Yes. He's always underfoot, underweight, under furniture, under my skin ...' Jared looked wounded. 'I'm sure you wonder why I have a Yorkie.'

'It had crossed my mind.' She was doing her best not to smile; if she once started, she was afraid that she'd never be able to stop laughing. 'Now if it had been a Siberian husky, or a wolfhound, or a Doberman——'

'Underdog was a gift.' He turned to the man who was waiting in the door. 'Peters, would you put this animal away somewhere? Under a box in the basement, perhaps.'

'Let me have him.' Gayle slid her hand into Jared's to

cup her palm under the dog's stomach. He had stopped barking by now, and the bright eyes turned to study her with amazing intelligence in their depths. Under the soft, curly coat was a wiry body.

Perhaps he's only a mechanical toy after all, Gayle thought bemusedly, and wondered just who had given Jared a dog. Someone with a sense of humour, that was apparent. She couldn't think of a single one of his women friends who would have seen the joke.

Peters had broken into a grin. 'Welcome to Pino Reposo, Miss Bradley. Lunch is ready—may I take your coat? and the dog, of course.'

Underdog protested with vehemence, but he was carried off down the hall unceremoniously. 'Something about you has inspired fierce loyalty there,' Gayle said, looking up at Jared through narrowed eyes.

'And you're wondering what it could possibly be,' he said. 'Let's have lunch while you think about it.'

She patted her hair back into place and looked around the entrance hall, trying not to stare. But this was so much different than anything she had expected that she couldn't help herself. The hall stretched the whole width of the house, but it was just a few feet deep. It was furnished only with large green plants, a couple of small benches, and a stunning piece of sculpture. The floor was brick-red quarry tile that seemed to stretch out forever. But what really caught her eye was the wall of glass opposite the entrance doors, for beyond it lay a courtyard, entirely enclosed by the house, that contained pool, fountain, trees—a complete little park under a glass roof.

'It's beautiful,' she breathed.

'I'll give you the complete tour after lunch. But we can walk through the courtyard now if you like.' He pulled open a glass door.

She had prepared herself for a chilly breeze, but stepping into the courtyard was like walking into a greenhouse. The rhythmic splash of water from the

fountain soothed her jangled nerves. The scent of
flowers was a soothing lotion after the harsh winter
outside. 'It's a tropical garden in January,' she said. She
reached out to touch the bright leaf of a plant that had
spilled out of its container and down a rock wall, and
she looked up at Jared with the pleased smile of a child.

And then she froze as he bent his head to kiss her.

It was brief, almost casual, just the brush of his lips
against hers, the barest pressure of his hand on the
small of her back, holding her. In an instant it was over,
and he stepped back, an eyebrow raised. 'You'll have to
do better than that if you hope to convince Russell
Glenn,' he said casually.

'Why did you do that?' She was breathless with fury,
and the blood was pounding through her arteries.

'Mainly because Peters is watching us from the dining
room, and I thought he'd expect to see something of the
sort.' He didn't sound concerned. 'Also because I didn't
want to take you by surprise later, when Russell and
Krystal are here.'

'What do you mean—take me by surprise? You never
said anything about this . . .'

'I assumed that it would occur to you,' he said coolly.
'You are not stupid, Gayle. It is only to be expected
that an engaged couple will occasionally touch each
other, no matter who is in the room. It won't be very
convincing if you flinch every time I walk by you.
Which brings me to the real question—is it just me, or
are you always a cold fish?'

'I can't see that it's any of your business,' Gayle
snapped.

'Oh, but it is. I shall have to teach you how to kiss;
I've already resigned myself to that. But I just
wondered——'

'How much farther you will have to go? Don't worry,
Mr Logan. I'll play along as far as I must—and I don't
have to be taught to kiss, thank-you! But as far as the
rest, it couldn't make any difference to you if I was

frigid! Because you will never get a chance to find out,' she added.

He was shaking his head. 'There is no such thing as a frigid woman,' he said firmly. 'You've just run into a clumsy man along the way.'

'I didn't say I was frigid! I just said——' Gayle suddenly realised what a hopeless battle she was fighting, and gave up. 'Let's have lunch.'

He smiled. 'You're a practical woman. I like that. Very well. Lunch first, and then we'll start your sensitivity training.'

She scarcely tasted her food, though she was certain that it was very good. Peters looked unhappy about her full plate, and she tried to explain to him that she had simply lost her appetite. Jared only smiled and took her arm to show her through the rest of the house. She walked along quietly at his side, trying to ignore his presence, wondering when he would make another move.

Sensitivity training, she thought, and could have screamed. Jared Logan was just about as sensitive as an aircraft carrier.

He ignored her silence and talked gently as they walked around the house. The courtyard formed the only hallway, and every room opened on to it. In the bedroom wing, each room had its own small sitting area looking out on to the courtyard, and there were so many of them that Gayle lost count.

'Why don't you put numbers on the doors?' she asked. 'Or you could paint them different colours, so your guests don't get lost.'

'It's really not that big a house,' he protested. 'Five guest bedrooms, plus my private wing, library, game room, living room, dining room——'

'Not exactly your average tenement,' she said drily.

'Would you like to see my rooms? No? I thought not.

If you ever change your mind, feel free to use the sauna or the jacuzzi.'

'I'll remember that.'

'You can trust me, Gayle,' he said earnestly. 'I have no intention of seducing you. It would cause far too many problems in the future.'

'That's comforting,' she murmured. She was holding on to her temper with great effort. He didn't need to make it so brutally plain that he had no personal interest in her, she thought. It was quite obvious to her that a man who had taken his choice from among the nation's loveliest women wasn't tempted to try his luck with Gayle Bradley.

And frankly, she told herself, she wasn't flattered by his assumption that if he paid any attention to her at all she would tumble into his arms. Her spine stiffened. Jared Logan just might get the surprise of his life, she reflected.

He took her into the living room. 'The Glenns should be here any minute now,' he said. 'They're renting a car at the airport.'

Gayle wasn't listening. Her eyes had instantly focused on the framed drawing on the far wall. She crossed the room to look at it. Then she said, with a note of wonder in her voice, 'No wonder you were surprised to see the Dali in my apartment.'

'It was a bit of a shock,' he agreed. 'This one could be a companion to it.'

'This is an even nicer one than mine.' She pointed. 'It has all the symbolism. I didn't know you collected Dali.' She looked up, with a sudden warmth in her eyes.

'I don't, actually.' He sounded apologetic. 'My mother gave me that last Christmas. She told me it meant that time is slipping away from me, and said I should make it a point to look at it every day.'

'She's right, you know. The clock face melting down into a puddle, and the stone tower crumbling——'

'I always thought she just made that up.'

'Come on, Jared, don't you have any poetry in your soul? Any imagination?'

'Sorry. Just computers. And don't blame my early upbringing; she really tried. From the time we were babies she dragged my brother and me through every art museum in New York City in rotating order, one a week.'

'And?' Gayle prompted.

'I like Frederic Remington's cowboys,' he offered hopefully. 'But probably only because they're cowboys.'

'What about the sculpture in the front hall?' she challenged, certain that she'd caught him this time.

He grinned. 'Sorry, Gayle. It came with the house.'

From somewhere near the kitchen came the shrill bark of the Yorkie, and then Underdog tore across the courtyard and hauled up short at the glass doors leading to the entrance hall, waiting impatiently for Peters to catch up with him and let him through.

Jared swore. 'Someday I'm going to barbecue that dog.'

'He's sweet!' Gayle protested.

He stopped short and stared at her. 'I should have known it,' he said. 'When it comes to useless animals, you're a marshmallow. I'll be lucky to get out of this mess without at least two stray cats and another mutt on my hands.' Without a backward look, he started for the entrance hall.

Gayle followed and bent to scoop up Underdog. The Yorkie struggled to get loose; it was like juggling a greased pig.

Peters had already opened the double front doors, and she shivered just a bit. But it wasn't only winter air that sent chills all over her body, Gayle thought. It was anticipation—she was scared to death.

Russell Glenn was coming up the walk. He looked bluff and hearty, with a red face and a little too much weight around the midsection. He was very much as she had pictured him from the 'phone conversations she'd had with him.

Beside him was a slim figure in a fox jacket, her head bent against the wind. She didn't look up till she was inside, and then she was laughing as she pulled the fox hat off and let blonde hair spill down over her shoulders. Her eyes were bright blue and her cheeks red from the cold.

Gayle didn't have to look up at Jared to see what he thought. She could feel the tension that coursed through his body.

Her head started to ache, and her fingers clenched in the Yorkie's long, soft hair. It isn't fair, she moaned to herself. Krystal Glenn was without doubt the most beautiful girl Gayle had ever seen. And it didn't take a genius to figure out that Jared Logan thought so, too.

CHAPTER FIVE

GAYLE stood at the top of a hill which overlooked Pino Reposo, and looked down at the house as it drowsed in the weak sunlight of late afternoon. The air was cold and crisp on her face, and the scent of pine and spruce stung her nose. The hillside was quiet, almost as if she had passed back in time a hundred years. She might have been alone in the frozen landscape, except for the hawk that circled above, looking for any stray fieldmouse which might have wandered out in the cold afternoon.

And then a giggle came from behind her, shattering the quiet perfection of the landscape, and she looked over her shoulder with aggravation.

Krystal Glenn, bundled into a bright red goosedown jacket, was trying to climb the little hill. Just as Gayle turned toward her, the girl's skis oozed out from under her, and she went down in a pile in the snow. It was as ungraceful an action as Gayle had seen all weekend from the lovely Krystal, and for one brief moment she had to fight down laughter.

Then Jared stooped to boost the girl back to her feet, and suddenly Gayle didn't feel like laughing any longer as she saw the smile on his face and the way Krystal was leaning on him.

She'd seen enough of that all weekend, she thought. Krystal had been hanging on Jared's arm within minutes of her arrival on Friday, and she'd been there ever since. The only thing that had changed today was the setting. Krystal had never been on cross-country skis before, and she was using it as an excuse to keep Jared next to her.

If she hadn't had that excuse, Gayle was sure, Krystal

64

would have found another. Gayle wished that she dared just go away. After all, what was the point in staying around for a whole Sunday afternoon of this? Jared certainly didn't seem to need her presence. He was dealing quite well with Krystal on his own.

It didn't help her attitude, Gayle thought, that Krystal Glenn spoke computer like a native. Gayle had thought that she herself had a fair knowledge; two years of working in the industry had made bits and bytes and bauds no mystery. But her job was to spell the words properly, and most of the time it didn't matter if she really understood them. Krystal breathed computers.

And Jared seemed to love it. The two of them had talked away hours with new applications for Logan computers, while Gayle had spent her time chatting idly with Russell Glenn and wondering if Jared had known that Krystal was a computer freak.

Not that it mattered, of course. The farce was almost over. Gayle dug her poles into the snow and pushed off down the hill. The short, stubby cross-country skis didn't react quite like the downhill ones she was used to, but the cold air brushing her face brought back a hint of the thrill of the resort slopes. She wondered what Krystal would have said if Jared had suggested some real skiing.

You're being a little unjust to the girl, Gayle, she told herself. You weren't so great on skis the first time either.

Her momentum carried her halfway up the next hillock, and when she climbed to the top of it, Pino Reposo was spread out right below her. One more easy run and she'd be there.

She turned to see where Jared and Krystal were. 'I can't make it,' Krystal was gasping. 'I'll just walk.'

'That's harder than skiing,' Jared warned. 'Without the skis, you'll break through the surface and be up to your knees in snow.'

And ruin the trail for every other skier who comes along, Gayle thought resentfully.

'I'm so hot,' Krystal complained. 'I can't go on.'

Jared didn't sound sympathetic. 'I told you not to buy the down jacket.'

'But you look frozen!' Krystal wailed. 'How can you stand to be out here in just a sweater and those silly earmuffs?'

'It isn't just a sweater. It's layers of sweaters.' Gayle thought that he sounded a bit impatient. 'You should have listened to Gayle and borrowed the clothes she offered you.'

Goodness, Gayle thought. I can't believe my ears. My wardrobe is actually getting a recommendation! Privately, she thought Jared looked great in his blue and white sweater. And she'd bet her last dollar that it wasn't any cheap imitation of Scandinavian wool, either.

She stopped to tuck her hair back up under her own wool cap. It did sound silly to Krystal, she supposed, that three sweaters could be warmer than any winter coat. But that was Krystal's problem. She didn't want to listen, and expecially not to Gayle.

The air of competition had crackled around the girl since Friday, when she had taken one good look at Gayle in the entrance hall. If I hadn't been wearing Jared's ring, Gayle thought, she'd have ignored me entirely, or treated me as a mere nuisance. But since she couldn't pretend that I wasn't there, she started a war.

One more dinner to get through, Gayle reminded herself. One more evening. One more breakfast, and Russ and Krystal will be on their way to California, and I can go back to being plain old Gayle Bradley.

And with a suddenly lighter heart, she pushed off down the hill, her skis spraying snow as she came to a stop at Pino Reposo's front door.

She left the skis on the doorstep, and was shedding hat, gloves, sunglasses and sweaters as she went. Russell

Glenn came to the door of the living room, a glass in his hand. 'Did you lose Krys and Jared out there?' he asked genially.

Despite the fact that his spoiled daughter was making life miserable for Gayle right now, she had to admit that there was something likeable about the man.

'They're coming. I think we wore Krystal out this afternoon.' Gayle stretched, and had to admit that she'd be feeling the effects tomorrow herself. It had been her first time on skis all winter, and cross-country seemed to use a different set of muscles.

He laughed. 'It's a good thing I stayed home, then. You wouldn't have wanted to carry an old man back to civilisation.'

'Nonsense. A friend of mine pulled a tendon in his knee last winter, and he skiied ten miles back to town. He said it wasn't something he wanted to repeat, but he couldn't have walked out.'

Russell shuddered. 'I'll stick to golf, thanks.'

The front door opened, and Krystal said, 'Thank God! You'll never get me on those things again!'

'You haven't seen Colorado till you've been down the slopes at Aspen or Vail,' Jared told her. 'This was just a warm-up.'

Krystal wailed, and Russell chuckled and clinked the ice in his glass. 'Want a drink, Gayle?'

'After I've put my hair back up.' She ran an experimental hand over her head. Taking off her cap had pulled most of the pins out, and now half of her hair had tumbled down her back.

'Don't,' Jared said. He had come into the living room almost silently, leaving Krystal still struggling out of her coat in the hall. 'I like it down.' He pulled out a loose pin and the rest of her hair cascaded around her shoulders.

'But it's such a mess——'

He didn't seem to be listening as he scooped up a handful of the shiny stuff.

'It's so heavy,' she whispered. 'And it needs brushing——'

'So we're all a little bedraggled. Russell doesn't care,' Jared said. He put a light kiss on the tip of her nose. 'Have a drink like a good girl. You can brush your hair later.'

She nodded. She wished that it wasn't necessary for him to touch her like that; even the teasing kiss bothered her, and she wished that he would stop. It was like being on stage with a bad script, she thought, wondering how to make the audience believe in the play.

Then she looked up and saw Krystal, who had paused in the doorway just in time to see the kiss. The hatred that flashed in the girl's eyes stunned Gayle.

'So what do you think of cross-country skiing now?' Jared asked, and Gayle pulled her thoughts back from the girl.

Russell put a china cup in her hand, and she took a long, grateful drink of eggnog. 'It's easier than downhill,' she said, 'and probably less dangerous. But it isn't nearly the thrill.'

'I can't believe you've never been on cross-country skis before,' he said. 'And you call yourself a Colorado girl——'

'I was never willing to settle for second best,' Gayle returned with a smile.

'I suppose you've skiied for years,' Krystal said sweetly. The tone of her voice made it sound as though Gayle was eligible for a senior citizen's pass on the slopes.

'You could even say decades.' There was just as much sugar in Gayle's voice. 'I broke my leg on a beginner's slope at Winter Park when I was six.'

Krystal tossed her head. 'I suppose anything you do for that long becomes second nature. I found it that way with a surfboard. Though of course,' she laughed merrily, 'I didn't start twenty years ago.'

Gayle gave her points for that one.

'I never could get the hang of surfing,' Jared said comfortably. He pulled off a sweater and tossed himself down in a deep chair.

'Oh, I'll teach you next time you're in California,' Krystal said eagerly. 'It's easy, really it is. Anyone with as much natural grace as you should have no trouble at all.'

Gayle almost choked on her eggnog. But it was true; Jared did move with the grace of a jungle cat, even if it sounded a bit silly to hear Krystal saying it.

'And I'll keep trying to ski,' Krystal said. It sounded almost like a vow. 'After all, if I'm going to live in Colorado, I won't want to be left out for half the year.'

Gayle did choke that time. She coughed, set her cup down hastily, and tried to recover her poise.

Krystal was watching her maliciously. 'Didn't Daddy tell you?' she asked then. 'I've decided to stay in Denver and run Softek. I've always liked the programming end of the business better than any other, and now that I'm through school, I can really concentrate on it.'

Gayle's eyes went instantly to Jared, but he didn't seem surprised at the announcement. What, she wondered, would this do to his plans? Would he give up on Softek? Or would he reconsider the advantages of marrying Krystal Glenn?

After all, Gayle thought, Krystal is a lovely child. And she had left no doubt in anyone's mind as to what—and who—she wanted.

Gayle had put her hair back up when she dressed for dinner. She didn't care what Jared had said; she'd wear it as she liked. Ten to one, he wouldn't notice anyway, she thought. He had probably only commented about it there in the living room because at that moment it was a way to demonstrate their affection to Russell Glenn. She didn't want to embarrass him, or herself, by appearing to take him seriously.

And she had been right, she thought a little resentfully as she walked across the courtyard to her room later that evening. He hadn't said a word about her hair, or her dress.

Why did I even bother, she wondered, thinking about the last week when she had frantically searched the stores for some new, colourful clothes. And then she answered her own question: she had planned to shock Jared with her sudden blossoming into colours, had hoped to please him by impressing his guests.

Instead, Krystal's vivid reds and hot pinks and bright greens made Gayle feel insipid. Beside that tropical flower, she felt like a washed-out, droopy carnation. Of course Jared hadn't noticed her. There was nothing to notice.

At least I made the best effort at it that I could, she told herself. She didn't know that the cold fresh air of afternoon had left her brown eyes full of sparkly life, and that the new dress, the colour of ripe peaches, brought out the tinges of red in her hair and the creamy tones of her skin.

Russell had already gone to his room, and Krystal and Jared were still in the living room, having a nightcap and finishing their discussion of memory chips in the new Logan computer. Krystal had started the discussion over the soup, and Jared had continued it through dessert and coffee.

And as for what they discuss when they've finished with the computer, Gayle thought crossly, I don't give a darn!

She strolled through the courtyard, in no hurry to go to her room. Sleep had eluded her the past two nights, and she had no desire to spend more hours staring at the ceiling above her head. She paused beside the fountain and let her fingers trail through the rippling water, watching as the droplets sparkled against the padparadschah ring gleaming on her finger.

It was just as well she liked the ring, she thought, because it looked as if she'd be wearing it for quite a while to come. If Krystal stayed in Denver——

For the first time, Gayle stopped to think of what that blithe announcement would mean to her. Instead of the deal that Jared had half-expected to strike over the weekend, they were in a worse position than they'd been on Friday. And instead of a three-day masquerade, they were stuck with one that might drag on for weeks, until something happened. Until Russell Glenn decided to sell Softek after all, or until Krystal gave up and went back to California——

Or until Jared decided to acquire the company the easy way.

Gayle sighed, pulled her hand out of the cool water, and walked straight across the courtyard to her room. Suddenly she wanted to be alone, to know that no one would intrude.

Peters had discovered within hours of her arrival how much Gayle loved to sit by a fire, and each night of her stay she had come back to her room to discover a small, neat blaze on the hearth. She smiled fondly. He was really a dear. She wondered why he continued to put up with Jared Logan. 'Perhaps he's hiding from the FBI,' she jeered at herself and put another small log on the fire.

As the fire crackled into life, Underdog raised his head from the blanket that half-concealed him, his bright eyes begging Gayle to hold him. That had got to be a habit, too, to find this little bundle waiting for her beside the fire.

She curled up on the loveseat in front of the blaze and sat there in the half-dark, watching the firelight sparkle on the baguette diamonds in her ring as Underdog licked her fingers.

Voices drew her attention to the window a little later. Since the lights were off, she hadn't bothered to draw the curtains across the glass doors that faced the courtyard. Now she didn't have to move in order to see Jared, with Krystal hugging his arm, crossing towards the guest rooms.

So Krystal won this round, Gayle thought. She bit her lip and told herself that it would do no good to be angry about it. But she was furious. Didn't Jared have enough sense to realise the danger he was putting himself in, by going to Krystal's room tonight? The little vixen had probably planned it that way, perhaps even set it up with her father.

And whatever happens, it isn't any of your business, she told herself sternly. If Russell Glenn bursts in on them, and demands marriage to save Krystal's honour——

'What honour?' she asked herself cynically.

She crossed to the curtains intending to close them so that she couldn't see what happened. After all, it was none of her business.

Then a dark figure appeared just outside the window, and she stifled a scream. Underdog started to bark.

The fire flamed up again, and she opened the door. 'I thought for a second that you were a ghost come down from one of the abandoned mines,' she said, relieved.

'Not a bad idea for a Hallowe'en costume,' Jared said thoughtfully. 'If you aren't in a hurry to go to bed, can we talk for a while?'

Gayle felt colour sweep over her face at his unintentional phrasing. He saw it and grinned. 'Sorry. That did sound like an invitation, didn't it?'

'Rather,' she said tartly. She led the way back towards the fire and reached for the switch on the reading lamp that hung above the loveseat.

'Don't,' he said. 'We don't need the lights.' Underdog scrambled across the cushions and across to Jared, stretching himself furiously in an effort to reach his hero.

Gayle shrugged and curled up on the end of the loveseat. 'So what do you want to talk about?'

He sat down beside her. 'I need to be in the office early,' he said. 'Can you be ready to leave by seven?'

'Of course.'

He stretched his feet out towards the fire, clasped his hands at the back of his neck, and looked at her curiously. 'Does anything upset you, Gayle?' he asked. 'Does anything ever make you lose your composure?'

'Not very often.'

'Isn't that a dull way to live?'

'No. I like my life just the way it is. Will Russ and Krystal be leaving that early?'

'Krystal won't see the light of day till ten, but since they're only going to Denver, it's hardly goodbye forever. I gave your love to her a few minutes ago, and we'll see Russell at breakfast.' He yawned and stretched an arm out over the back of the couch. It lay within an inch of her shoulders.

Gayle stayed absolutely still. 'I'll be glad to get in early. My work is piled up, too.'

'The sneak preview party for the new computer?' His hand brushed the loose hairs at the back of her neck.

She ignored him, and said, 'It takes a lot of organisation.'

'I don't think I've ever realised before how valuable you are with these things,' he said. 'What's that perfume you're wearing?'

It took her an instant to change mental gears. 'It's called shampoo,' she said with dignity.

His hand wandered over her hair, and a pin tumbled into her lap. She put up a hand in protest.

'Don't,' he said. 'I'm just checking out what you told me.'

'Jared——'

Her hair spilled down, and he held a handful of it to his nose. 'You're right,' he said, sounding a little surprised. 'It is shampoo.'

'If anyone should know, it's me,' she said drily. 'Now may I put my hair up again?'

'No,' he said, and his lips brushed her throat. 'I prefer you to look a little mussed when I kiss you. It makes you seem much more human.'

Gayle's fingers clenched on the arm of the loveseat, but there wasn't time to argue.

His lips were warm and gentle, caressing, stroking. He kissed the corners of her mouth, the arch of her eyebrow, the hollow of her cheek. Gayle neither moved nor responded; she was passing the time by counting each separate caress. She was rather pleased to notice that his kisses tickled a little, and that she was able to remain totally in control of herself, though her heart was beating just a little faster than usual.

He released her and sat back in the corner of the loveseat, an eyebrow raised. 'Do you realise that in this entire weekend you haven't kissed me back once?' he asked curiously. 'I must have kissed you a dozen times, and——'

'Twenty-seven,' she said, before she had a chance to think about it. 'Eighteen just then, and——'

He didn't seem to appreciate the tally. 'Do my efforts amuse you?'

Gayle shrugged. 'I never thought about it. It just seemed to be part of the job. And by the way, why did you kiss me just now? There's nobody here to impress.'

'Call it an experiment, if you like.' There was a brief silence. 'All right, Gayle. Is it you or me?'

'What do you mean?'

He sounded impatient. 'Do you treat your boyfriend like this?'

She leaned forward to poke at the fire. 'Does it wound your ego because I'm not falling all over myself to get into your bed?'

'Of course not.' He sounded amused.

'You just never quit, do you? You can't believe that there is a woman on this earth who might not be attracted to you.'

'As a matter of fact, I prefer it this way. It's much less complicated. But it doesn't look very convincing.'

'Why don't you just tell everyone that I prefer to do

my lovemaking in private?' Gayle was angry now. 'And while we're on the subject, it must not look too good to have you hovering over another women, either.'

'Are you jealous?' He sounded satisfied.

'Of course not. But it does make me wonder why we continue to play this game, when you are so obviously interested in Krystal Glenn.'

'That's simple. I still don't want to get married, you know.'

'Ah! Now I understand. You've made it all perfectly clear!'

He just grinned at the sarcasm in her voice. 'Well, it's true,' he said mildly. 'I'm just being friendly to her.'

'You have a different definition of it than I do.'

'Yes, I know. You don't even have a kiss to spare for a friend.' There was a long silence, and then Jared asked, his tone gentle, 'What is it, Gayle? You're a pretty woman. I can't believe there's never been a man in your life, and yet you don't date——'

'Of course I do. There's Larry, remember?'

'How did you explain this to him, anyway? I'm dying of curiosity.'

'I didn't tell him anything. I didn't want to upset him.'

'Thoughtful of you.' He let the silence draw out till it was painful. Underdog, who had gone to sleep again, sighed and yipped a little. The fire crackled.

Gayle sighed. Jared was apparently going to sit there silently till he got some sort of answer. 'I was in love once,' she said finally. The words came painfully at first; she so seldom talked to anyone about Craig. 'He was my high school sweetheart. We were going to be married ...' She looked down at the padparadschah ring, thinking about the ring she and Craig would have chosen, if only there had been more time. The diamond would have been tiny, not much more than a chip, because they were saving to furnish their house. But it would have been a symbol of love. Suddenly the padparadschah felt heavy and uncomfortably warm on her hand, like a chain that held her fast.

'Did he find another girl?' Jared's matter-of-fact voice brought her back to reality.

'No. He died. Cancer.' She bit her lip. fighting back the tears. 'Seven years ago.'

'And you went into mourning from which you have never emerged.' The words were sympathetic, but the tone held a challenge, almost a note of irritation. 'Is that what you call love, Gayle, if it cripples the survivor?'

She looked up at him, anger sparkling in her big brown eyes. 'You can't know how it was,' she snapped. 'You weren't there.'

'No. And I never will be in that spot. I'm not foolish enough to let my happiness depend on any one person.'

She wanted to strike out at him, to scream at him that he had no right to tell anyone else how to live. If he wanted to pursue his dissipated path with one woman succeeding another so quickly that even he could not possibly remember all the names, that was his choice. But to tell her that she was wrong——!

But she didn't say it. She fought down the words, and finally said, in a taut little voice, 'At any rate, that's why I don't find you particularly appealing.'

'But you don't find me repulsive either?'

Gayle shrugged. 'I'm rather lukewarm on the subject, actually.' She expected that it would sting his vanity, perhaps even make him lose his temper.

But Jared merely smiled. 'I don't take it personally. You're lukewarm on men in general, aren't you? It must be damned lonely, up there in your ivory tower. Poor Larry.'

'I don't need a man in my life,' she said stiffly.

'Granted. I don't NEED women, either, but I certainly do enjoy having them around.' He leaned back, tenting his fingers together and looking her over thoughtfully. 'Tell you what, Gayle,' he said finally. 'We're stuck with this little game for a while longer. Let's at least have a bit of fun while we're at it.'

'I doubt that your definition and mine are anything alike. And I do not appreciate being thought of as nothing more than a sex object.'

'Or perhaps,' he mused, ignoring her interruption, 'we should call it a scientific experiment. Bring Gayle Bradley back to life—that's a good motto. Maybe even teach you to play the field and enjoy it——'

'I don't want to play the field!'

He looked her over, his eyes dark and appraising. 'Why not?' he asked mildly. 'Are you afraid that you might find out that you've wasted the last seven years?'

'I haven't wasted anything.'

'Or are you just chicken? I won't take advantage of you——'

Her temper flared. 'You couldn't seduce me if you tried!' she snapped. She saw the spark of satisfaction in his eyes, and only then did she realise that she had issued a challenge.

'Prove that you're untouchable,' he said, very softly. His voice was little more than a breath. 'Why don't you kiss me this time, Gayle, and prove to me that you haven't forgotten how?'

Her whole body was throbbing with anger. How dare he say those things to me, she thought, and make the most beautiful thing in my life look cheap!

'Get out, Jared,' she said. 'Get out of here before I start to scream.'

He shrugged and stood up lazily, then bent over her as she sat stiffly upright on the loveseat. 'Goodnight, Gayle,' he said pleasantly, putting a gentle kiss on the nape of her neck. 'That's still the darndest shampoo I've ever smelled.'

He picked up Underdog, who protested sleepily. Then he was gone, absolutely unhurried, leaving her sitting there in the darkness by a dying fire, uneasily aware that he had left because he chose to, and not because she had ordered him to go.

Gayle sat there for a long time. Finally, she crept into her big bed, and for the first time in years she cried herself to sleep.

CHAPTER SIX

THE drive back to Denver was silent. Gayle studied the highway speeding by as if she expected to have to draw a map of it. Jared tried various subjects, but she refused to respond to his blithe conversation.

Finally he asked, 'Are you just pouting? Or are you afraid that I'll try the seduction routine?'

'Neither,' Gayle snapped.

'Don't worry about it. In a sports car it's darn near impossible.'

She bit her tongue to keep from answering that, knowing that he simply wanted to provoke her to a response.

'Besides that,' he added, 'girls in black don't turn me on. It's like flirting at a funeral—definitely out of place.'

She didn't answer that either, but she was grimly glad that she had returned to her regular office uniform. If it irritated him, it would at least help prevent a repetition of last night. Just thinking about the loveseat and the dying fire sent cold chills up her spine. Anything she could do to prevent a recurrence of that was well worth the effort.

Thomas, down at the information desk in the lobby, looked startled when they came in so early and together, and by the time they reached the executive floor, Gayle's nerves were in shreds. She gave a sign of relief when she was safely in her own office. The last thing she needed was for it to be public knowledge that they'd spent the weekend together . . . no matter how innocently.

The cheerful companion of early morning disappeared abruptly as they reached the office; Jared told her that he didn't want to be disturbed, and he closed his office door without waiting for an answer. That was one problem solved, she thought. She knew this distant mood well; when he acted like this, he was usually solving an abstract engineering problem—and sometimes he wouldn't talk to anyone for days.

A little peace and quiet, Gayle thought. That's what this office needs.

What would happen, she wondered dreamily, if she walked into his office right now, without even bothering to knock, and announced that this farce was finished, that she would quit her job rather than continue to play this role, that as far as she was concerned Jared Logan and Softek could burn for eternity——

She didn't know what he'd do. But she did know that he'd have an answer, and that she would be the one who yielded. His method might be quiet charm, it might be an appeal to company loyalty, it might be outright blackmail, but in the end Gayle would stay. She might as well keep her dignity intact, and not make a scene of it, she told herself.

The telephone on her desk was chiming, and she looked at it with foreboding. Sometimes the office was like Grand Central Station, and in her state of mind this week, she couldn't handle that.

The caller was Natalie Weston. As soon as Gayle answered, the woman's voice hardened. 'I want to talk to Jared,' she demanded.

'I'm sorry, Mrs Weston. He's taking no calls this morning. If you'd like to leave a message——'

Natalie laughed harshly. 'Are you joking? Leave a message with you? How do I know you'll give it to him?'

'You don't,' Gayle told her sweetly. 'But I will.'

'I'll just bet! Now that you're engaged to him, you must really enjoy answering his 'phone. You won't tell him I called or anything——' Natalie sounded frustrated.

Gayle knew the feeling. When Jared wanted to be out of touch, he could be extremely hard to reach. The love nest had a telephone, but he rarely gave out the number. Pino Reposo was nearly as difficult; Gayle herself had had trouble getting that information from him. And at the office, all calls had to go through her— No wonder Natalie was ready to have apoplexy.

'Mrs Weston, I will give him the message.'

'Perhaps I should just come down there and sit till he goes to lunch!'

It would do her no good, Gayle thought, since Jared usually left through the back door. She shuddered at the thought of Natalie Weston staring at her all morning. 'Is there a number where he can reach you?' she asked politely.

Natalie finally gave it to her, grudgingly. It must have been hard for the proud beauty to descend to begging, Gayle thought, but she felt little sympathy. If Natalie didn't want to play by the rules, she philosophised to herself, then she should not have chosen as a playmate the man who wrote the rulebook.

'If you try to stop him from calling me——' Natalie threatened.

'Why should I do that?' Gayle asked her sweetly. 'As his future wife, I have no reason to be jealous of you, Mrs Weston.' She put the 'phone down hard, instantly regretting that she had been pushed into losing her temper. No matter how much Natalie Weston deserved it, there was no excuse for a professional secretary to treat a caller like that.

By the time this episode was over, she thought glumly, she'd be lucky to have any shred of composure left. She remembered, longingly, the peaceful succession of her days before Jared Logan had turned her life into a tornado. She hadn't known, then, just how lucky she was.

She sighed and turned to her own morning's work. The new computer would be unveiled in less than two weeks, and the sneak preview party was Gayle's job. The food, the flowers, and the string ensemble were already arranged, but there were a million details. At least, she thought, this was the kind of work she was used to. It was a whole lot better than playing hostess to weekend guests!

It was almost noon when she looked up at a young woman who had come in, very quietly, from the hallway.

The woman breathed subtle elegance. Gayle had been around long enough to recognise mink when she saw it, and the coat draped over this woman's arm didn't have to display its label to brag of what it was. Her emerald suit showed off a slender figure to perfection. Her blonde hair needed no chemical help to maintain its flaxen colour. And her deep green eyes studied Gayle with an air of watchfulness.

She looks suspicious, Gayle thought. Of me. But that's ridiculous! Why would a woman like her be wary of me? Why would she take any notice of me at all?

As she stood up to greet the visitor, Gayle's eye caught the flare of the padparadschah ring on her finger. Of course, she thought, that's it. This must be another of the women in Jared's past. Rumour certainly travels quickly.

'May I help you?' she asked.

The woman had also seen the ring. Her eyes raised speculatively from it to Gayle's face. 'You must be Gayle Bradley.'

Gayle nodded. I've heard this voice, she thought. But which woman does it belong to?

Then the woman smiled. It was the smile of a gleeful child, and her big green eyes sparkled. 'Tell Jared I'm here to see him,' she said, and it was at once a command and a gentle suggestion. Gayle had never heard anything quite like it.

She started to tell the woman that Mr Logan wasn't seeing anyone today. But just then the door of the inner office opened and Jared leaned out. 'Gayle, would you bring me——' He stopped dead as he saw the woman.

The woman tossed the mink coat across a chair, crossed the room to him, and stood on her toes to put a kiss on his cheek. 'Hello, dear,' she said.

Gayle had almost stopped breathing. She felt a little as if she was window-peeking.

'You haven't been in Denver in a year,' Jared pointed out. 'And your regular skiing trip isn't till next month. You aren't going to make me believe this is a coincidence, so tell me—what brings you out here?'

The woman laughed. 'I overheard part of a very interesting conversation on the 'phone the other day, so I came out to see what mischief you were up to this time. Aren't you going to introduce me to your fiancée, Jared?' When he didn't answer, she came back across the room to Gayle, her hand outstretched. 'I'm Elizabeth Logan,' she said. 'And I'm delighted to meet you, Gayle.'

Of course, Gayle thought. That crisp, clear voice—she had heard it a hundred times over the telephone, but never before in person. No wonder she had had trouble placing it.

Jared's sister-in-law was here, checking her over. And what would the verdict be? Gayle's knees were weak and her fingers trembled as she extended her hand across the desk. Elizabeth took it with a warm smile.

'I suppose the whole family knows about this by now,' Jared drawled.

Elizabeth raised an eyebrow. 'She doesn't look like the sort of girl you'd want to hide in a closet, Jared,' she chided.

'That's not what I asked.'

'Do you really expect me to keep secret the fact that you've finally found the woman of your dreams?'

Jared groaned. Gayle didn't. A groan would not have been enough to express what she felt right then. She toyed with the idea of committing suicide with her letter opener, and then gave it up reluctantly.

'I did tell you once that you should watch out for brunettes,' Elizabeth told Jared over her shoulder. 'I'm taking her to lunch, by the way. I want to warn her about you.' She picked up the mink. 'Get your coat, Gayle. I want to hear ALL about it.'

Gayle stared at Jared, shock and horror still mingled on her face. Get me out of this, her big brown eyes pleaded.

He shrugged his shoulders as if to say, What can a mere man do against Elizabeth?

'Be a darling, Jared,' Elizabetn advised him. 'Make a dinner reservation for the three of us tonight.'

'Better yet,' he said, 'I'll just come along to lunch.'

'No, dear,' Elizabeth said. She sounded very much as if she was talking to a three-year-old. 'Lunch is for girltalk only. You'd be bored.' She took Gayle's coat off the hanger and handed it to her.

Jared's eyes met Gayle's, and he shrugged again. She interpreted his look with a sinking heart. She was on her own, and it was up to her to convince this inquisitive young woman that all was delightful in their own personal Eden. There was no mistaking the threat in Jared's eyes; at all costs, the fiction was to be maintained. What was it he had said? Never share a secret with anyone who doesn't need to know it. As far as he was concerned, there was certainly no need to bring Elizabeth Logan into it.

Elizabeth chatted gently until they were in the lift. Then she started to laugh, and looked at Gayle with that gleeful smile. 'I can't tell you how delighted I am,' she said.

'It's—pleasant to get such a warm reception,' Gayle managed to say.

'How did you manage to pull it off? I have to admit that I gave up on Jared as marriageable material long ago.'

Gayle waved a hand and tried to look modestly unwilling to discuss the matter.

Elizabeth just smiled, and Gayle's heart sank. It was going to be very difficult to keep this woman guessing, she thought miserably. Jared Logan is going to pay for getting me into this . . .

It was the dead of winter outside, but inside the sleek little restaurant it was springtime. Gayle retreated behind the oversized menu and tried to restore her badly shaken poise. She would need every ounce of it, she thought, if she was to get through this meal. She ordered crêpes, stuffed with chicken, and topped with a mushroom sauce. At least they were easy to eat, and if she couldn't swallow, she could push the food around on her plate and make it look as if she was eating.

'The crêpes for me, too, please,' Elizabeth told the waiter. 'And bring us a bottle of white wine, to celebrate. When is Jared taking you East to meet his parents, Gayle?'

Gayle swallowed an ice cube. She clutched at her throat, her eyes watering. 'He—I don't—He hasn't said,' she stammered finally.

There was sympathy in Elizabeth's gaze. 'I suppose he could invite them out here,' she said finally. 'They'd drop everything to come and meet you, that's sure.'

'You actually told them?' Gayle's voice was a mere horrified whisper.

The green eyes were sympathetic. 'As a matter of fact, I didn't,' Elizabeth admitted. 'But the first thing you need to learn about the Logans is that there are no secrets. And why Jared wants to keep you hidden is beyond me, anyway—unless he just doesn't want to look a fool.'

'For becoming engaged to his secretary, I suppose,' Gayle said. Suddenly, illogically, she was angry. So he'd be a fool to look at me, is he? she was raging inside. She wished that she had worn something besides black this morning. She could hear the report that would go back

East with Elizabeth Logan—the poor thing, how could Jared ever be serious about her . . .?

Elizabeth was startled. 'Heavens, no! It's just that he's said so many times, and so definitely, that he would never marry. When he turns up with a fiancée he'll never hear the last of it. Oh, Gayle, I didn't mean anything uncomplimentary about you!' She looked stricken, as if she half expected that Gayle would stalk out of the restaurant.

'I can't imagine that his parents would be best pleased.' Gayle sampled her wine and kept her voice level with an effort. How silly it was to feel furious about it. She should be thanking heaven that she wouldn't have that problem to face . . .

'Oh, Helene would be a perfect lady,' Elizabeth drawled. 'And then as soon as Jared had turned his back, she'd be doing cartwheels in her drawing room, Honey, you are so much different than Jared's usual——'

'Is that another compliment?'

Elizabeth smiled. 'As a matter of fact, yes. If it tells you anything, you're the first one I've ever invited to lunch.'

'Well—thank you.' Despite herself, her attitude was warming. There was something about this woman that drew Gayle.

'I was a little surprised by what I overheard on the 'phone that day, but I wasn't shocked. Not that I ever expected Jared to see the light. After a man has chased after gorgeous dolls for years—or worse yet for his ego, had them chasing after him—one doesn't expect him to recognise real beauty.'

Gayle laughed. 'I'm glad to have a champion, but you don't have to perjure yourself to get into my good graces, Elizabeth.'

She was subjected to a long, cool green stare. 'If ever a woman was suitable to share Jared's breakfast table——' Elizabeth began, and then broke off.

'Though it is only fair to warn you. Living with a Logan is an exhausting proposition, and marriage is a life sentence. When you have children, don't expect them to be like you. Oh, they might look like you—but in every way that counts they'll be their dad all over again. There's no escaping it.'

The sudden image that swam before Gayle's eyes, of a half-dozen miniature Jared Logans, made her dizzy. 'I wouldn't want them to look like me.'

There was a sudden, deafening silence. Then Elizabeth said, 'You're serious, aren't you? You don't think you're pretty.'

Gayle tried to laugh it off. 'The world's most beautiful women have walked through my office. I have no illusions left.'

'And wait till you see them in ten years,' Elizabeth said brutally. 'They'll be hags. As for you, when you're fifty, you'll be able to pass for thirty-five.'

'Do I have to wait so long?' Her tone was flippant.

'But black isn't your colour.'

'That's what Jared keeps telling me. He offered to buy me a new wardrobe.'

'And you turned him down?' There was a gleam of humour in Elizabeth's voice. 'No wonder he decided to marry you.'

Suddenly it didn't matter any more. Jared would not be pleased by what she was about to do, and he would probably think of some outrageous punishment. But suddenly it was very impprtant to Gayle that she not lie to Elizabeth any more. This, she felt somehow, might be the beginning of a friendship she could treasure. She did not want it to be based on a lie.

She put her fork down and said, 'Jared would kill me for telling you this——'

'Oh, in that case,' Elizabeth said comfortably, 'I think I should hear all about it.'

So Gayle told her about Softek, and Russell Glenn, and Krystal, and the padparadschah ring that was only a bribe. She thought for a moment that the woman hadn't comprehended, because only cool amusement gleamed in Elizabeth's eyes as she sipped her wine and listened.

But when the recital was finished, she said cheerfully, 'I thought there was a strong aroma of cod about this whole affair. That's why I didn't call Helene with the wonderful news.' Sudden disappointment flared in her eyes. 'And now, in all conscience, I can't tell her at all. Darn.'

'Thank you,' Gayle said fervently. 'You don't know what a relief that is for me.'

Elizabeth didn't seem to hear. 'It wouldn't be fair to raise her hopes, when I know they're going to be dashed——' She stopped suddenly, her green eyes lighting. 'Or will they? You've told me about Jared's reasons for this little performance. But what about yours? What do you think of Jared?'

'He's a good employer—he's fair, but he's hard to work for——'

Elizabeth sighed. 'I meant as a MAN, Gayle.'

Gayle shrugged. 'He's all right, I suppose. I never thought of him as a man.' It was true, strictly speaking, but it made her feel like a dunce to say it that way. 'I'm quite happy with my life as it is,' she said a little stiffly. 'I don't plan to marry, and so I don't assess every man I meet as a candidate.'

Elizabeth thought about that, and then went straight to the heart of the matter. 'You aren't secretly in love with him, are you?'

'With Jared?' Gayle was horrified. 'Of course not!'

'Good. You've worked for him for a couple of years, haven't you?' At Gayle's nod, she went on thoughtfully, 'And for all that time you've arranged his dates——'

There was a cynical note in Gayle's voice as she added, 'Reserved the tables, ordered the tickets, sent the flowers on the morning after . . .'

'I'm stunned, I thought Jared had enough class to at

least do that much himself,' Elizabeth mused. She pushed her plate aside with sudden decision, and leaned forward to study Gayle. 'I think it's about time he got paid back, don't you? Now is your chance to teach Jared Logan a lesson for the sake of all women.'

'I don't think I could do that.'

'Of course you can. Follow your instincts, Gayle—fight dirty.' She signalled to the waiter. 'Bring us a pot of coffee, please,' she told him.

Gayle was uneasy. 'I don't know what you expect me to do,' she began.

'What any red-blooded woman would love to do to that man. He's treated you like dirt for two years. Make him pay!'

'But it's my job——' Gayle protested.

'From what I can see, he can't run that business without you. At this moment, he needs you more than you need him.'

It was true enough. If he fired her, there would be havoc in the office. And it was very tempting.

Elizabeth shrugged. 'So if he fires you, come to Chicago. I can find you a job in a minute.'

I owe Jared Logan one, Gayle thought. There was a long silence as she studied her new friend. 'I may take you up on that,' she said finally, 'if this doesn't work. What do I have to do?'

Elizabeth's face seemed to light up. 'First you finish your coffee,' she ordered. 'And then we are going over to Larimer Square—you are authorised to charge things to his credit cards, aren't you?'

'Of course, but——' Gayle was horrified. 'That's stealing!'

'He told you he'd buy you a wardrobe,' Elizabeth pointed out. 'You've simply changed your mind about accepting it. Besides, I'll bet we could shop all day for less than he spent on that ring you're wearing.'

Gayle cupped a protective hand over the padparadschah. 'I have no idea how much it cost.'

'And it's probably a good thing you don't know, too,' Elizabeth told her unsympathetically, 'or you'd have been afraid to wear it.'

'That much?'

'Just don't go lock it up in a bank vault,' Elizabeth recommended, 'or I'll be sorry I told you. Do you always wear your hair that way?'

'Usually.' Except when Jared starts pulling pins out of it, she thought, and then was very glad that she hadn't said it. She would have felt a little silly, telling Elizabeth about that.

'A good basic haircut could do wonders,' Elizabeth mused. 'That and the clothes——'

It was time to bring this game to a halt. 'You're being a little silly,' Gayle said firmly, 'if you think that a haircut and a new dress will make any difference. It certainly isn't going to set Jared back on his heels.'

'Not by itself, no,' Elizabeth said comfortably. 'But you new attitude will. If you're going to act the part of his lady love, then you deserve the perks. Make him take you to the theatre, to the opera—if that's your style, of course——'

'The art museum opens a new show next week,' Gayle mused.

'He'll hate it. But with any luck, he'll find out what it's like to be used—wined and dined and dropped. It might even make him a bit more human.'

'The next Denver symphony concert,' Gayle added.

'No. He has season tickets, so that wouldn't bother him.'

'Nevertheless, you're getting the idea,' Elizabeth applauded. 'Now let's go use up his credit.'

Gayle came back to earth with a bump, and the wispy dream of arriving at the concert hall in Jared's Jaguar, instead of her usual taxi, faded away. 'I have to go back to work,' she said. 'I've been gone too long now——'

Elizabeth laughed. 'Jared knows me better than that,'

she said.. 'He knows that I wouldn't dream of bringing you back before five!'

She told herself afterwards that it was the wine. She wasn't used to drinking much at all, and certainly not three glasses of wine with lunch. But deep in her heart she knew that was only an excuse. Part of her wanted to go right along with Elizabeth's plans, and so she wavered only a moment before she put herself into the capable hands of the hair stylist. And after that, the manicurist. And after that, the make-up adviser. And after that——

The day sped by, and so did the bills. She hesitated over the first one, but Elizabeth egged her on. From then on, Gayle signed Jared's name without a qualm, telling herself that if she was going to be in trouble for this stunt, she might as well make it big trouble.

They worked their way back towards the Logan building, buying winter clothes, spring clothes ('You should have something to remind you of him as the seasons go by,' Elizabeth advised), shoes, handbags, hats.

'I've never worn hats,' Gayle said. 'I've always been afraid of them.'

'With those cheekbones and the great big elfin eyes? Promise me that you won't waste yourself like that any more, Gayle. Look at that gorgeous painting in the gallery window.'

Gayle started to protest, because it was getting late. Then, as she looked up at the window, a painting displayed there seemed to draw her in. It was a seascape, with waves crashing against a rocky shore, so realistic that the surface of the painting looked wet. She felt oddly breathless as she stood there in front of it. 'Why haven't I ever seen that before?' she asked no one in particular. 'I walk past this window twice a day.'

Elizabeth shrugged. 'It probably hasn't been there long. Want to go in?'

Gayle stared into the scene, feeling the contrast between the crashing violence of the waves and the deserted calmness of the shore. It would change moods with the time of day, she thought, knowing that if she owned it, she would spend hours studying it.

'No,' she said firmly. 'I don't want to find out that I can't afford it.'

Elizabeth laughed. 'That's a loser's attitude. But I suppose you're right—it's getting late, and Jared will be fuming.'

'He probably has been for hours.' She caught a glimpse of herself in a shop window and was startled by her new look. They'd cut barely an inch from her hair, but the master hand on the scissors had released a natural wave that had delighted the stylist. He had left it loose around her shoulders, trimming the top into a windblown cap of curls that framed her face. Between that and the new make-up, which made her eyes look huge and mysterious, Gayle felt like a different woman. Which, she supposed, was exactly what Elizabeth had intended.

'On second thought,' Elizabeth said, 'let him fume for a few minutes longer. Let's go in here.'

Gayle looked up at the sign and stopped dead. 'Not on your life,' she said firmly. 'This is carrying things a little too far, Elizabeth.'

The blonde woman laughed. 'No, I don't expect you to buy anything at the stork shop,' she said. 'This one is for me. I just want to see what I'll be wearing next spring.'

She was fingering a delicate green maternity dress when Gayle recovered her voice. 'You're pregnant?'

Elizabeth nodded. 'Now we've shared all of our secrets,' she said. 'Would you look at this? What kind of exhibitionist would wear a purple jogging suit when she's pregnant?'

'Especially one with pink trim. I won't tell a soul about the baby, Elizabeth.'

'Don't worry about it. I expect Helene already

knows. Come to think of it, the day I went to the doctor she just happened to call—I think the woman is psychic when it comes to grandchildren.' She pushed a dress away with a contemptuous finger. 'I hate having no waistline, and not being able to see my feet, but here I am anyway. Logan charm is deadly, you know.'

Gayle remembered business conferences she had attended. 'I've seen Jared use it.'

'Well, don't say you haven't been warned that you're playing with fire.'

'But you're in love with your husband. Of course you find him charming.'

Elizabeth was shaking her head. 'It makes no difference,' she warned. 'And if you think Jared can charm the birds from the trees, wait till you meet his father. The Logan boys are only beginners, compared to that old pro.'

Gayle privately thought that Elizabeth was underestimating herself. Perhaps Logan charm was contagious; Gayle felt a little as if she was basking under a sunlamp, just from being around this Logan for an afternoon.

Elizabeth had gone on to a row of negligées. 'Can you believe this? Who would want to wear white lace when she looks like an elephant? White lace is what got me into this predicament.' She sighed. 'Well, I refuse to buy a single thing until I absolutely can't fit into my regular clothes. We'd better go back to the office. I wonder if he made dinner reservations.'

'He has probably forgotten how,' Gayle muttered. She pulled the collar of her coat up and nestled her chin into it. Shock at herself, and at what she had allowed Elizabeth to talk her into doing, began to settle like the chilly wind into her bones.

'Elizabeth,' she said finally. 'You and Jared will have a lot to talk about—family matters, I mean. You won't want me along at dinner, will you?'

'Are you trying to run out on me? Of course I want

you there; that's the whole purpose. You're still my sister-in-law to be, aren't you?'

'Not quite.'

'Until you tell Jared to jump off the highest Rocky Mountain, that's what you are, and officially I don't know anything different. I plan to play it dumb and straight.' Her eyes were sparkling. 'It should be a great deal of fun to watch him squirm—don't you think?'

CHAPTER SEVEN

ELIZABETH was as good as her word. Her role as the doting, curious but never prying sister-in-law was so superbly done that Gayle caught herself believing it. And Jared looked so uncomfortable that she had trouble stifling laughter.

Until, over dessert and coffee at The Pinnacle, Denver's most exclusive new top-floor restaurant, Elizabeth and Jared mentioned that the annual Logan family skiing trip was just four weeks away. Gayle's eyes almost popped at that news.

'And everybody is coming out this year,' she said faintly.

Elizabeth smiled. 'Oh, yes. We all go to New York at Christmas, and everyone joins Grady and me in Chicago for a week in summer. But the first week of March is Jared's time to play host to the masses out here. And this year, my dear, no one would dream of missing the trip—and you.'

There was a rare gleam of humour in Jared's eyes as he watched Gayle absorb the news. If this farce isn't over by the end of the month, she was thinking we'll have more Logans to convince—and two of them will be Jared's parents.

She had completely forgotten this annual pilgrimage to the ski slopes. Every year she arranged for the lift tickets and the lodge. It always fell to her to take care of the details, and the reservations had been tucked away in her desk drawer for months. But Jared's guests never showed up at the office. They went directly to Pino Reposo, or even straight to Aspen or Vail. It's no surprise that you forgot all about them, Gayle tried to tell herself. And you have only your rotten luck to blame. This whole mess could just as well have happened in July, when there was no snow, no skiing trip, no Logans coming to visit . . .

'Are you going to make your mother wait four whole weeks to meet his girl, Jared? Shame on you,' Elizabeth scolded.

Jared shrugged and smiled. 'She's waited years. Another month won't hurt her.'

Waiting certainly won't break my heart, Gayle thought. With any luck, Russell Glenn would sell Softek by the end of the month, and then Jared could explain this uncharacteristic lapse to his family all by himself.

'When is the wedding, Jared?' Elizabeth asked. 'You'll need to give us plenty of warning, you know—we will all have to juggle our schedules so we can be here. And shall I tell Grady to start practising? He almost dropped my wedding ring—I'd hate to have him lose Gayle's. You do want him to be the best man?' Her eyes were big, green, and intent on Jared's face over the rim of her coffee cup.

Jared didn't flinch. 'Actually, we hadn't discussed when and where. Until this new computer is launched, I frankly don't have time to worry about a wedding.'

'I'll tell him not to hold his breath,' Elizabeth murmured. 'In the meantime, Gayle can be planning all those glorious details. If you'd like a ringbearer, dear, my son is available.' She looked thoughtful. 'But I wouldn't recommend him.'

A sudden touch of mischief promoted Gayle to say, 'It would be nice for him to have some cousins.'

Elizabeth's eyes sparkled. 'He'd love it. Grandma's attention is a little overwhelming at times. Jared, your mother will be delighted at the prospect of more grandchildren.'

Jared looked as if his collar had suddenly gotten a little too tight.

Gayle sipped her wine and looked out the window,

trying to ignore the conversation. The lights of the city spread out below them in a blanket of gold. The slow motion of the revolving restaurant had already carried them in one full circle over the panoramic Denver skyline. To Gayle, it felt like a dozen. In fact, she was beginning to feel just a little seasick about the whole affair, and she was regretting the impulse that had made her take Elizabeth into her confidence.

No, she told herself stoutly. Elizabeth would be saying the same things even if she hadn't known the truth. It wasn't Gayle's fault if Jared was uncomfortable with the questions. He should have anticipated them, and he might as well get used to it.

Just as she might as well start looking now for another job, she thought. If he ever found out the full extent of what she had told Elizabeth, she'd never work at Logan Electronics again, that was certain.

He'd been in such a temper when they'd finally got back to the office that Gayle wouldn't have been surprised if he had fired her on the spot—Elizabeth or no. It hadn't helped the situation that Natalie Weston had been sitting in the outer office, bullying the girl that the secretarial pool had sent up to take Gayle's place. Jared had been furious, and though Elizabeth's laughing presence had kept him from saying everything he wanted, Gayle had no illusions. The flames might be banked down right now, but at the first opportunity, she would hear about it.

She only hoped that when the time came she could hang on to her temper. Up until last week, she thought with amazement, she would have had no trouble keeping silent when she was reprimanded. That was what a professional secretary did, and she certainly deserved this lecture. But now, she didn't know if she could prevent herself from yelling right back at him . . .

'I wonder if the engagement will make next week's news magazines,' Elizabeth speculated, and Gayle swallowed hard. 'It might even raise the price of Logan

Electronics stock, Jared. To say nothing of your father's bank stock—the dynasty continues, you know. Shall I call my friend at *TIME*, do you think? After all, this is an event.'

'I'll announce it, when I'm ready for it to be official,' Jared said curtly.

'Sorry to disillusion you, dear boy, but the moment the ring goes on the finger it's official. And you certainly can't keep that one a secret.' She gestured toward the padparadschah ring on Gayle's finger.

Gayle allowed the waiter to refill her wine glass, ignoring the dark look that Jared threw at her. She didn't really care what he thought. She was in no danger of getting drunk, and if she wanted another glass of wine that was her business.

Though, she thought cynically, she could be forgiven if she did get smashed. She'd never been to this shiny new restaurant before, but in the three months since it had opened atop Denver's tallest new building, she had made enough reservations to seat the Seventh Cavalry. The Pinnacle had rapidly become Jared's favourite; if he didn't take the latest lady of his dreams there, then he ordered a catered supper for two at the love nest. It was that simple.

Yes, Gayle thought, she had a right to be annoyed at him for bringing her here. For all she knew, every woman in the place had been introduced to it on Jared's arm. Was that why he'd done it, she wondered—to remind her that she, too, was a very temporary measure, despite the ring she wore?

'Where are you going to live?' Elizabeth asked. 'Will you keep Pino Reposo? It's so far from Denver.'

The very thought struck at Gayle's heart. 'Sell that gorgeous house?' she asked. 'I wouldn't allow it!'

Jared looked amused. 'That sounds pretty definite to me, Elizabeth. But we haven't had a chance to talk about it. Where do you want to live, Gayle?'

She didn't miss a beat. 'Wherever you are is good

enough for me, dear.'

He grinned. 'In that case, we could just redecorate the love—the penthouse.'

Gayle hadn't missed his slip, and she wasn't about to let it pass unremarked. 'I'm sure it could stand a massive overhaul,' she said acidly. 'But I think we should look at the new condos they're building. Up high, of course, so there's a good view of the mountains on clear days.'

'You could remodel the penthouse,' Elizabeth said. 'I agree that it would take far more than new wallpaper. But it certainly has the view, and some of the rooms are so big that you could cut them in half. You could move walls—all kinds of things. And it would be handy for Jared.'

Not even to Elizabeth would Gayle admit that she'd never been inside Jared's love nest. 'Perhaps we should do that,' she mused. 'After all, if we were to buy a condo, the penthouse would just sit there—unused.' She raised her eyes to Jared's and was astonished that there was no gleam of laughter in his. But then, she thought, perhaps he didn't see the humour in the suggestion— Don Juan being forced into retirement, as it were.

'Well, it certainly resembles an echoing tomb now,' Elizabeth murmured. 'You could do wonderful things with it—put in a full master suite with another bedroom and a dressing room——'

'Hold it right there,' Jared ordered. 'No apartment of mine will ever have more than one bedroom. It's a waste of space.'

Gayle felt hot colour rising in her face.

'Which is why I'm staying at a hotel,' Elizabeth pointed out. 'Perhaps the girl would like some privacy now and then, Jared. At least allow her a boudoir all to herself. Are you going to stay on as Jared's secretary, Gayle?'

'We—hadn't talked about that, either.'

Elizabeth smiled, a slow, sultry smile. 'I'd ask what

you DO find to discuss—but I don't think I want to hear about it.' She skipped on, blithely ignoring Gayle's discomfort, and started to quiz Jared about Natalie Weston.

By the time Gayle focused her attention back on the conversation, Elizabeth was shaking her head sadly. 'The woman bleaches her hair, Jared. I thought you had better taste—at least in your ads. Why don't you use Gayle? I'll bet that she photographs superbly.'

'Not in a hoopskirt, thanks,' Gayle put in.

'Gayle makes her contribution in other ways,' Jared added, with a sidelong look at her. 'As a matter of fact, I'm thinking of naming the next computer after her— because it, too, is a model of reliability and efficiency.'

Gayle bit her tongue to keep from answering with a sarcastic gibe of her own. She was being paid back, she knew, for the remark about the love nest being abandoned, and she deserved it. Then she noticed that the woman at the next table seemed to be listening to the conversation. Which one of Jared's harem is she, Gayle wondered. She reached across the table to slide her hand under his, and said with a sugary smile, 'How thoughtful of you, darling. Remind me to tell you, when we're alone, just how that makes me feel—to have a computer for a namesake.'

He shrugged off the jab and signalled the waiter to bring the bill. 'Unless you want another cup of coffee, Elizabeth?' he asked. 'Gayle doesn't need another glass of wine.'

She started to do a slow burn, and then, as he reached for his wallet, the full impact of what she had done that afternoon finally hit her. If he pulls out his business credit card, she thought, I have to stop him. After her shopping spree, the card must be barely worth the plastic it was made of, and it would be embarrassing for them all if the waiter was the one who broke the news to Jared that his charges exceeded his credit limit.

Elizabeth intercepted the waiter. 'This one is on me,'

she said smoothly, and the gleam of cash passed from her hand to the waiter's.

Jared scowled. 'I've never let you pick up a restaurant tab yet, Elizabeth, and I don't intend to start now.'

She smiled. 'Tonight you have no option,' she said sweetly. 'We ruined your charge accounts this afternoon. Ran them to the limit.'

He sounded a little stunned. 'All of them?'

'Every one we could get our hands on,' Elizabeth murmured. 'It was great fun . . . Shall we go?'

Elizabeth was going back to Chicago on the morning flight, so they said goodbye when they dropped her off at her downtown hotel. When they came back to the Jaguar after walking her into the lobby, the silence was so thick that Gayle could hardly breathe, and without Elizabeth's quiet support, she felt twelve years old and horribly alone.

'I'll take a cab home,' she offered in a small voice.

Jared didn't dignify that with a comment, just raised a dark eyebrow and put her into the car. They didn't speak again until he'd parked in front of her apartment building.

Gayle reached for the door handle. 'I'll take the clothes back,' she said miserably. 'And I'll pay for the other things—the things I can't return. The haircut and the manicure . . .'

He didn't seem to hear. He sat there silently, like a stone statue, for a moment that seemed to stretch into eternity. Then, abruptly, he got out of the car, came around to open her door, and, with a firm hand on her elbow, walked her towards the door.

'I'll come in early tomorrow,' she added. 'I'm really sorry about just walking out of the office today. A good secretary doesn't behave like that——'

'Stop chattering, Gayle.'

'I don't know what happened to me,' she said. She felt wretched about the whole affair. Suddenly she didn't care how angry he became, if he would just say something. It was the brooding silence that wore on her nerves.

He didn't sound interested. 'Aren't you going to offer me a cup of coffee?'

'Just coffee?' Then she bit her tongue, hard. By now it should be obvious to her that he had no designs on her virtue, and never would have.

He angled a look down at her, his eyes hard, and for a moment she was afraid that he was going to use those exact words. Her hands were shaking. 'Of course,' she said very quietly. Neither of them spoke again until they were inside her apartment.

He followed her to the kitchen, as if afraid that she might disappear if he let her out of his sight. The tiny corridor kitchen was scarcely big enough for one person, and the addition of a very large, very irritable male made Gayle so nervous that she almost dropped the glass pot. She was trembling so badly that coffee grounds scattered like dark snowflakes across the kitchen counter.

Jared watched her struggle for a moment, then swore under his breath and took the spoon out of her hand. With an angry economy of motion, he started the pot brewing. Then he leaned against the counter, folded his arms across his chest, and asked, 'Are you approximately sober?'

Gayle's nervousness burned up in fury. 'I am entirely sober!' she snapped. 'I had two glasses of wine all evening, for heaven's sake!'

'Good. I wouldn't want you to have a hangover tomorrow at the office.'

'Look, Jared, I don't blame you for being angry. But I said I'd take the things back——'

'Do you really think I'm angry about the clothes?' He shrugged. 'I told you to get yourself some new things.'

'I didn't stop with a few,' she admitted. 'It was

hundreds of dollars worth——'

'It didn't take Elizabeth long to teach you how to act like a member of the family,' he said drily. 'Keep the clothes; it's no big deal.'

She said, hesitantly, 'But if you're not angry about the clothes, then what——'

'Gayle, if you leave that office for an afternoon again without getting someone in from the typing pool, so help me——'

Of course, she thought. It wouldn't be mere money. A man who lived as he did wouldn't even notice the bills she'd run up that afternoon. But interfere with the smooth running of his office, and there was hell to pay. Suddenly she felt a deep, irrational desire to strike back. 'It just goes to show you what a crazy idea this marriage talk is,' she murmured. 'Logan Electronics couldn't function without me.'

The gleam of anger in his eyes startled her. 'Don't bet on it,' he warned, and his voice cracked like a whip. 'And don't forget that you're only wearing that ring for my convenience. There is certainly nothing personal about it.'

'You needn't warn me not to take you seriously, Jared. I'm in no danger—frankly, I can't imagine a worse fate than being married to you!'

'Just remember that. No woman has ever threatened my independence, Gayle—and no one ever will.' The words rang out like a challenge in the quiet kitchen. In the silence, the coffeemaker sighed as it finished the cycle.

'How unfortunate for you,' Gayle said quietly. She reached for two mugs and filled them.

'How do you mean—unfortunate?'

'You said I must be very lonely.' Automatically she spooned cream and sugar into her coffee. She looked up at him, directly and unsympathetically. 'But at least I loved, and I was loved. You don't know what the word means.'

'Oh, yes, the boyfriend who died. Are you sure that he isn't just a convenient excuse to avoid men?'

'I'm certain.' She led the way into the living room, glad to be out of the close contact of the tiny kitchen, and curled up in a corner of the couch.

'Is this him?' Jared gestured with his coffee cup at the enlarged snapshot on the mantel.

Gayle looked up at it too, though she had long since memorised each detail. She had taken the photograph about a year before Craig's death. They had packed a picnic that day and gone up into the mountains, hiking back along a hidden trail to a stream untouched by tourists. There they had eaten their lunch, waded in the water, napped in the crisp air. It had been their last time to play in the wild. After that, he'd been too exhausted by the cancer that haunted his body.

'That's him.'

He picked up the photograph. 'What was his name?' His voice had a hard edge; it was more demand than question.

She didn't want to answer. It was none of Jared's business, after all. But she could think of no adequate reason to refuse. 'Craig,' she said softly.

'You really cared about him, didn't you? I can hear it in your voice.'

'Did you think I was joking about it?'

He raised an eyebrow and studied the snapshot. 'He doesn't look like the sort who could inspire eternal devotion,' he jibed, and set the photo down hard on the mantel.

'Looks aren't everything. Jared, I'd rather not talk about Craig any more.'

'Was he a good lover?' The edge was still there in his voice, under the casual tone. He came across the room to her.

Gayle was furious. 'It is not necessary to reduce everything to sexual terms, Jared.'

He let the silence lengthen, his midnight-blue gaze

intent on her face. 'Does that mean you never even slept with him?'

Gayle felt the colour rise in her face, and tried to fight it down. She stared at the bottom of her cup, and finally set it aside.

'It does.' The tension had suddenly disappeared from him, and he sounded fascinated with his discovery, like a child just starting to investigate a new toy.

'I can't see that it's any of your business whether I slept with Craig or not.'

'Can't you?' he said, obliquely, and set his cup down on the coffee table. 'How do you know what you're missing? Are you positive you're sober, by the way?'

'Stone cold. Why?'

'Because I don't want you to forget this.'

He moved so suddenly that even if there had been a place to run to, Gayle could not have moved. Before she even saw his intention, he had pulled her so close that the breath was smashed from her body. His hands roved with a casual familiarity that brought hot colour to her cheeks. She tried to pull away, but the hard strength of his arm held her like a steel cage.

'What are you doing?' she demanded. 'Take your hands off me! Jared, leave me alone!' She was having trouble breathing. His mouth was moving with agonising slowness up the sensitive skin of her throat, and his moustache tickled. 'You just can't stand to be around a woman who isn't falling all over herself to get into your bed, can you?'

His voice was a little muffled as he said, 'It's not that. You're a challenge, Gayle. You keep telling me that you're untouchable, but I don't believe you. Those feelings aren't dead—I think you've just let them all go to sleep.'

His mouth seemed to raise blisters on her skin as he nibbled at her throat, teasing his way down the deep neckline of her dress. Gayle's breath was coming in tight, painful gasps. 'You certainly aren't Prince Charming, coming to wake me up,' she snapped.

He laughed and let her go. 'I was right,' he said smugly. 'You're nothing but a self-righteous little prude, Gayle. One case of puppy love, and you think you're an expert, qualified to tell the rest of the world how to carry on its affairs——' He picked up his coat.

She had fled across the room. She turned, her fists clenched at her sides, so angry that she could hardly speak. 'A prude, am I?' she snapped. 'Well, hang on to your socks, Jared Logan. You have a lesson to learn.'

He was standing in the centre of the room by then, and he tossed his coat back on to the chair and put his hands on his hips. 'So teach me,' he invited. 'I don't mind being treated like a sex object.' -

She crossed the room to him, feeling as if she was taking the last few steps to the guillotine. But it was too late to back down now; the challenge had been issued and accepted, and if she didn't carry it through she would be left no peace. So she looked up what seemed an immense distance, into eyes so dark blue right now that they looked black, and let her hands skim over the smooth silk of his shirt to clasp at the back of his neck.

It was the first time she had ever been so close to him of her own will, and she stood there a moment, studying his face, the laugh lines that clustered around his eyes, the threads of silver that had started to appear at his temples. He had always been a handsome man, she thought a little bemusedly, but the distinguishing marks of age would make him even more so. When he turned sixty, woemn would still be throwing themselves in front of him . . .

'You're getting silver hairs,' she whispered.

'It's culture shock. When Elizabeth started talking about kids, I could feel myself turning grey.' He raised an eyebrow. 'Stop stalling, Gayle. You said you had something to show me.'

She took a deep breath, stood on her toes, pulled his head down, and kissed him, full and warm.

He stood easily, hands still on his hips, absolutely unmoved, and let her kiss him. His lack of response piqued her, and she threw all caution to the winds. He wasn't going to get by with laughing at her, she told herself, and ignored the deeper anger that was bubbling in the back of her mind. She arched her body against him, tangled her fingers in his hair, and let the tip of her tongue tease against his lips.

'You changed shampoos,' he said.

And that was all the whole episode meant to him. Gayle was furious. 'They washed my hair at the salon before they cut it,' she said curtly, and started to turn away.

He pulled her tight against him again. 'It isn't much fun without a little co-operation from the other party, is it, Gayle?'

'I didn't expect it to be fun. Aren't you going to rate me on your own private scale?' Her voice was heavily sarcastic. She struggled to break free, but it was like breaking out of jail with her bare hands.

He shrugged. 'If you insist. Average—not bad for an amateur. With some practise, you could acquire a professional polish——'

Suddenly, she found herself on the couch, being propped to a half-sitting position with cushions. He had moved so quickly that she didn't even know how she had got there. She started to struggle, and Jared held her down. 'Co-operation, that's the key,' he said.

'You keep saying that you don't want to sleep with me——'

'If I wanted to sleep with you,' he said, very quietly, 'you'd be in the bedroom right now, I'm just going to give you a quick lesson.'

'And once you've taught me to kiss, you'll leave me alone?' she asked drily.

'The challenge will be gone, you see.' He didn't give

her a chance to argue. 'Call it a fringe benefit for Larry.'

This was a different kind of kiss, she thought dreamily, a gentle, teasing assault on the senses. He feathered gentle caresses on to her face, on the tender triangle under her ear, down her throat. When he turned his attention back to her lips, his tongue teased gently until, despite herself, she relaxed, opening like a flower under his sensual siege.

'That's better,' he murmured huskily, and explored her mouth with slow sensitivity.

He tasted like coffee, she thought vaguely. She was feeling just a little dizzy. Perhaps she'd had too much wine at dinner after all . . .

Her hand had slipped down on to his chest, and she could feel the steady thump of his heart under her fingers. Was it only her imagination, she wondered, or was it beating a little faster than a normal rate?

If he was, she didn't have the satisfaction of knowing. He gently let her drop back against the pillows, and stood up, running a hand through his hair. 'Not bad for a first lesson. I think you'll be ready for an exam by the end of the week. See you tomorrow at the office.' He was gone before she could answer.

Gayle propped herself up on one elbow and stared at the silent door. 'I'm glad he left,' she told herself crossly. 'I'm relieved that I didn't have to kick him out.'

But the words rang hollowly in the silent room.

CHAPTER EIGHT

THE glare of sun against snow sent brilliant light reflecting into Gayle's eyes as she left the Logan building. The day was bitter cold, and the wind seemed to slice through her wool coat. Thank heaven it was just a block to the little restaurant, she thought. Any further than that, and they'd have had to chip her out of a block of ice in the spring.

She stopped in front of the gallery window to admire the seascape, and then, with a shiver, walked on. The bright light today made the painting look like high noon on a misty day. The transformations it made under different lighting was the strangest thing she'd ever seen.

It took a moment to accustom herself to the dimmer light inside the small restaurant. Then she saw her brother waving from a table toward the back, and she hurried to join him.

Uneasiness tugged at her. What was it that Darrel wanted to talk to her about? He had surprised her that morning when he had called the office, and the invitation to lunch with him had come out of the blue—the kind of thing he seldom did.

Was something wrong at home, she wondered. After all, she had been out to the house for dinner with him and Rachel just a few days ago. Surely, if it had been any ordinary thing, he'd have told her about it then. But what if he didn't want to talk about it—whatever it was—in front of Rachel? Had something gone wrong with his marriage? Could there be a problem with little Amy? Or . . .

Oh, stop it, she told herself crossly. It was probably nothing at all; she was just being touchy. It was unfortunate for her, however, that he'd chosen this particular day for a heart-to-heart. The unveiling party for the new Logan computer would start at mid-afternoon, and it would probably continue to the wee hours of tomorrow morning. And on Gayle's desk there was a long list of things yet to be done, before the party began.

Darrel rose and pulled out her chair. 'Glad you could come, Gayle.'

'What's the special occasion?' She opened the menu and looked up at him across it.

He shrugged, but his eyes were watchful. 'I just decided it was time for our semi-annual private chat, without Amy wanting you to draw pictures and Rachel tugging you off to admire her new dress.'

'Sorry, dear, but your timing is off. You couldn't have chosen a busier day.' She spread her napkin out in her lap. The corner of it caught on the padparadschah ring, and she stole a look at Darrel, hoping that he hadn't noticed the gleam of the stone.

How could she have been so darn careless, she thought. She'd made it such a point, when she went to dinner with them last Friday, to leave the ring securely at the bottom of her handbag. It was easier that way; on her hand, it could never have escaped Rachel's sharp eyes, and the explanations would have gone on forever. It was much better, she thought, if they never knew about this mad engagement.

But today she'd been so busy that she'd forgotten all about the darned ring, and here she was wearing thousands of dollars worth of padparadschah and diamonds and pretending that nothing unusual was going on.

She slid the ring carefully off and dropped it into the corner of her handbag. Darrel was studying his menu, and she sighed in relief. She was safe, for the moment.

'Do you mean all the hullaballoo about the new

computer?' he asked. 'I read about it in last month's magazines.'

'That was only idle speculation. Today is the first time anyone outside the company will see it, and the atmosphere over there is pretty thick.' It wasn't that Jared lacked confidence in his new product; as a matter of fact, Gayle thought, it was one quality he had in super-abundance. But the suspense of the unveiling was enough to give them all ulcers. 'It won't actually be sold publicly until next month.'

'Tenderloins all right?' Darrel asked. 'It's the best thing they serve here.'

'Sure.' She put her menu aside. 'What is it, Darrel? What's wrong?'

'What do you mean?'

'You call me for lunch three or four times a year. Something has to be bothering you, or we wouldn't be sitting here. And besides that,' she pointed out gently, 'you don't usually spend your time tapping your spoon on your water glass unless you're deadly nervous.'

He looked down at his hand, as if surprised to find the spoon there. Then he sighed and put it down. 'You're right,' he admitted. There was another long silence. 'Have you seen Larry lately?'

'Not for—I don't know. Ten days or so. Why?'

'He fell for you pretty hard.'

'I don't see how he could. I saw him twice, and one of those was a ride to work. Have you suddenly turned matchmaker, too?'

He shifted uneasily in his chair. 'No, but—He's a nice guy, Gayle.'

'He's not my type.'

'So what is your type? Craig seems to be the only candidate, and he's dead.'

'I suppose I deserved that.'

'Rachel says you're trying to bury yourself with him.'

'Just because I'm not flitting from man to man, looking for a replacement? Look, you can go home and tell Rachel that much as I love her, I wish she would stay out of my business!'

'Sometimes we have to be told things that hurt, Gayle. And Rachel's right on this one. You're turning yourself into an old maid——'

'I loved Craig!'

'No,' Darrel said firmly. 'You loved the idea of being in love. You were nineteen years old, for God's sake. You've mourned him now for seven years. Isn't that long enough?'

'I've never met a man like him.'

'Waiting for another one like him would be an even bigger mistake.'

She stared at him for a long moment. 'And just what does that mean?'

'You're not the same person you were seven years ago, Gayle. A man like Craig——' He shook his head. 'I've never said anything to you about Craig before, because I hoped that you'd eventually see it for yourself. I didn't want to hurt you. But perhaps it's time that someone told you the truth.'

She was stunned. 'You liked Craig!'

'Sure, I liked him. He was an easy-going, fun-loving guy without a thought about the future. All play and no work.'

'That's not true. He had plans——'

Darrel went on ruthlessly. 'And did you see any evidence of him carrying them out? They were castles in the air, Gayle.' He let the silence draw out for a long moment. 'Why didn't you go to college?'

'Because he got sick——'

He shook his head. 'If it hadn't been that, there would have been something else. He didn't want you to go. He was afraid that you might find out that you wanted more than he could give you. You might even have discovered that dream castles are draughty, and then you might have wanted something a little more secure. You might have made some demands on him, then, like asking him to get a regular job, and——'

'I wanted to stay with him,' she said, softly. 'I wanted to spend every minute with him——'

'If he had really cared about you, Gayle, he would have wanted what was best for you.'

'But to go away to school——'

Darrel shook his head. 'You could have started college right there. You could have seen him every day, and still have been preparing yourself for a career and a life without him. You wanted an education. But he demanded that you be beside him every minute. He was afraid that if he let you out of his sight——'

'Stop it!' Her voice was little more than a cracked whisper.

Darrel looked at her sadly. 'You're a secretary today because Craig convinced you that it was the only proper job for a woman to have. You're still trying to earn his approval. But in spite of all your efforts to be what Craig wanted, in the last seven years you've changed. If he was to walk in that door right now, Gayle, in five minutes you'd see that I'm right. You'd tell him to take a long walk off a short pier.'

She stared down at the sandwich the waitress had just set in front of her, and pushed it aside. The very smell of it made her feel ill.

'But Craig is gone,' Darrel said, 'and he isn't coming back to show you what a jerk he really was. It's a damn shame, Gayle.'

'His life was wasted——' she said.

'And so you're wasting yours, as well.' He poured ketchup on to his french fries, and looked up with harsh sadness in his eyes. 'Now that I've said my piece, I'm done. You can walk out on me if you want—I will certainly understand. That's the risk I took when I opened my mouth.'

She shook her head. 'You're still my brother,' she

whispered. You're wrong, she thought, dead wrong—but you're still my brother. The only family I have . . .

Some of the tension seemed to go out of him. 'Sorry about ruining your lunch,' he said. 'I intended to hold off on the heavy discussion till after we'd eaten. It's a shame to waste a good tenderloin.'

She forced a shaky laugh. 'I suppose I'd better try to eat it,' she said. 'It's going to be a long afternoon.'

'Me, too,' he said. 'Two weeks' worth of work to do today, and going out of town over the weekend——' He snapped his fingers. 'That's the other thing I was supposed to tell you. Rachel asked if you'd come to dinner tomorrow instead of Friday. She's going with me to Phoenix for a conference.'

Gayle forced down a bite of the tenderloin. She supposed it was good, but it tasted like sawdust. 'She's got plenty to do. Let's just miss this week.'

'Hey, we really like having you come. I understand if you're mad at me, but——'

She tried to smile. 'It's all right, really. I have to cancel out sometimes, too, you know. Are you taking Amy along?'

He grimaced. 'More's the pity, yes.'

'Leave her with me. I'd enjoy having her for the weekend.'

'You don't know what you're letting yourself in for,' he warned.

This time Gayle's smile was genuine. 'If you're going to try to marry me off, Darrel, it's only fair to let me prepare myself for the experience.'

'That's true. At least when you have a three-year-old of your own, you'll know what you were getting into.' He reached across the table for her hands. 'Friends?'

She hesitated for a long moment, then her fingers clasped his. 'I think you're wrong, Darrel, but I understand that you said it out of love for me. I warn you, though, I don't promise to date Larry. There are limits.'

'Fair enough. Just think about what I said, that's all I ask.'

A hand came to rest on Gayle's shoulder. She jumped, startled, and felt the brush of a moustache against her cheek. 'Hello, darling. Sorry to interrupt, but when I see my fiancée I just can't stay away.' Underneath the charm in Jared's voice was a challenge.

Gayle put her hand over her eyes. This isn't happening, she told herself firmly. This is only an hallucination. It is not real.

Then she looked up at Jared, all six cynical feet of him, and sighed. 'Don't make a bigger fool of yourself than is necessary,' she recommended.

'I'll consider it. Are you going to introduce me, or shall I have to do it myself?'

Darrel had got to his feet. There was wary uncertainty in his eyes; Jared's expression was just as cautious.

Gayle waved a hand in a hopeless gesture. 'Jared Logan; Darrel Bradley. Darrel is my brother, Jared.'

'You said—your fiancée?' Darrel asked. He didn't offer his hand.

'Purely a temporary——' Gayle started to say.

'Just until the wedding,' Jared added cheerfully. Underneath was a thread of steel, a warning to Gayle. Admit no one to the secret who didn't need to know it, she thought. Her vocabulary wasn't sufficiently wide for her to have expressed her feelings just then, so she kept quiet.

Darrel turned piercing grey eyes to Gayle. 'I don't believe it,' he said. 'Why didn't you tell me, before I gave you that lecture——' He seized Jared's hand. 'I have to admit that I admire your taste,' he added with a grin.

Gayle grasped at a straw, and said, 'Didn't you say you have to be getting back to the office, Darrel?'

'As a matter of fact, I do. Look, after the weekend,

let's all get together. Rachel is going to be delighted to meet you, Jared.'

Gayle's head was throbbing. She closed her eyes to ward off the pain.

Darrel turned to her, his smile glowing. 'I thought you looked different—but I decided it was just the new haircut. Just wait, my girl—you are going to get a scold about keeping us in the dark, Gayle!'

'It happened just a few days ago,' she said, and stared up at Jared, daring him to contradict her.

'I see that you don't even have a ring yet,' Darrel said. 'I do have a client waiting for me; I have to run.' He dropped a kiss on Gayle's cheek. 'See you Friday when we drop the angel off. And I'm looking forward to knowing you better, Jared.'

Jared was thoughtfully fingering his moustache. 'Does he always chatter like that?' he asked.

Gayle gave him a long, cold stare, and didn't bother to answer. She reached for her coat.

'That look must mean I'm in trouble,' he hazarded. 'And what did he mean, you don't have a ring? What happened to it?'

Gayle ignored him. She pulled her gloves on slowly and carefully, paying close attention to each finger. If she hadn't, she would have hit him.

'At least come and say hello to Russell Glenn,' he prompted. 'If I hadn't been having lunch with him, I wouldn't have bothered you at all. But you have only yourself to blame. It didn't look good, my fiancée so absorbed in conversation with another man that she didn't even——'

'I am not your fiancée,' she said then, fury almost burning up her voice. 'I am tired of this ridiculous game. It is getting nowhere, and I am sick of being the one who——'

'Russell and I were discussing terms,' he pointed out gently. 'He's agreed to sell Softek.'

'Good. Then you don't need me any more!'

'It doesn't quite work that way. Krystal is still less than happy about it, and if she suspects that this whole thing is a farce, the deal will never go through. In fact, there's just one more small thing . . .'

'No! Whatever it is, no!'

'Need I remind you that if you mess this up——'

'So fire me!' For a moment, they were squared off. Gayle's breath was coming fast; she was trying to hold on to the last shreds of her temper.

Jared smiled down at her, and then bent to kiss the tip of her nose. His hand closed gently on her arm, but there was the promise of brute strength if he chose to use it.

She gave in. It was a hopeless battle, she knew; Jared would not hesitate to create another scene, and he absolutely refused to ever admit defeat. So she smiled at Russell Glenn, and murmured something sweet, and waited patiently on the sidewalk while the men said their goodbyes.

As soon as Russell had hailed a cab, Jared returned to her side. She shrugged away from his hand and set a fast pace for their walk back to the Logan building. By the time they reached the front door, she was breathing hard from the exertion. Jared didn't seem to notice.

She maintained the icy silence clear to the executive suite. But once the door was closed behind them, she turned on him, fury burning up any shred of common sense that remained. 'Why did you do that?' she demanded. 'Isn't it enough that half of Denver thinks I'm sleeping with you? Did you have to go announce it to my brother, as well?'

Jared shrugged. 'I didn't know he was your brother,' he pointed out. 'In fact, you never told me you had one.'

It was ridiculous for her to feel defensive, but she did. 'Why should I?' she asked. 'This stupid production was only supposed to run for three days—why on earth should you meet my family?'

'Listen, it wasn't my idea to drag it out for three weeks.'

'I know,' she said with sarcastic sympathy. 'It's cutting into your social life with a vengeance. Just how much longer do you think this is going to last?'

'We have to hang on for one more lousy week. Give or take,' he said, over his shoulder, as he started for his own office. 'Russ hasn't signed anything, and the deal can still go down the drain until he does. In the meantime, get that ring back on your finger where it belongs. And don't take it off again!'

'I don't think I can stand another week of this,' Gayle retorted as his office door slammed. But she didn't dare to defy him. She yanked her handbag open, reached for the padparadschah——

And her fingers closed on emptiness.

The sudden tightness in her throat was like a hand clenched there, and she fought for breath. 'I know I put it in my purse,' she said. It wasn't possible that the ring had disappeared; there was nowhere else it could have gone——

Unless she had missed the pocket of the handbag, and dropped it on the restaurant floor.

'Oh, God,' she moaned. Jared would kill her. No, she thought grimly, she'd kill herself and save him the trouble.

She upended the handbag over her desk blotter and shook it. 'Please, please, please,' she was thinking, her mind revolving like a hamster in a cage. If she begged hard enough, and was sorry enough about her carelessness, it might reappear——

One last shake, and light shattered off the dozen baguettes and gleamed from the padparadschah as the ring spun out of a corner of the handbag on to her desk. She picked it up with shaking fingers and sagged back into her chair, every muscle in her body limp.

I will never let it out of my sight again, she swore to herself. I will never take it off my finger again——

Jared reappeared in the door of his office. 'I'm going down to check on the——' He raised an eyebrow at the array of compact, change purse, cardcase, hairbrush, and assorted junk on her desk. 'If you don't have anything better to do this afternoon than clean out your purse——'

Gayle sat up and scrambled everything back into the bag. 'I have plenty to do.'

'Then let's start, shall we?' he said sweetly. 'I'll be back in a few minutes.'

It can't be too long for me, she thought. 'Is this ring insured?' she called after him.

He turned at the door. 'I don't bother with the small stuff,' he said, and went out.

Now I know I'll never take it off again, she thought. She slid the ring back into place on her finger, the cool platinum warming quickly against her skin as if it liked to nestle there.

Don't be silly, she told herself. It's only a ring.

She had to fight to keep her mind on her work, as she checked off the last-minute items on her lists in preparation for the party. Darrel's words kept drifting through her thoughts, his voice cold and almost harsh as he had said, 'You loved the idea of being in love . . . Dream castles are draughty.'

He was wrong, she told herself firmly. Her love for Craig had been a fine, wonderful thing, the warmest and best time of her life. If Craig had lived . . .

She was in the lift then, waiting patiently as it creaked down to the lobby, where the caterer's tables should be set up by now.

She looked at herself in the mirrored door. She was wearing one of the outfits she'd bought the day she and Elizabeth had gone on that crazy spree. The dark mahogany dress with its crisp white trim brought out the tinge of red in her dark hair, and the make-up techniques that they had shown her made her eyes look big and bright. The cloud of curls around her shoulders was so much easier to take care of that she wondered why she had kept her hair long and straight for so many years.

Because Craig had liked it that way, she realised. It hit her with the weight of a truck, which was silly. It was such a little thing. So what, if she had kept the same hairstyle for years?

What was it Darrel had said? 'You're a secretary now because Craig thought it was the only proper job for a woman.'

'That's not true,' she said aloud. 'I like my job.' But her voice was wavery.

She took a deep breath, and for the first time she let herself think about what her life would be like now if Craig had not died. How many moves would there have been, as Craig chased one dream after another? When she had been a teenager, it has seemed exciting—his unwillingness to be tied down to anything, the breathless anticipation of what lay around the corner. But what had been so stimulating then, now seemed like a hair-raising ride on a roller-coaster that had gone out of control. Craig had never talked about today, she realised. It was always next week, next year—someday.

'My God,' she said quietly, 'Darrel was right.'

And what would she have been doing, while Craig pursued tomorrow? Would she have followed him from vision to vision, in search of his perfect world? Or would she by now have told him—as Darrel had expressed it—to take a long walk off a short pier? By now, she thought, she could well be divorced and supporting herself anyway. And perhaps she would have had a child or two to care for as well.

There would have been no Dali prints hanging in her apartment then, she thought. There would have been no luxuries like membership in the art institute, and season tickets to the symphony ... Her luxuries would have been new shoes for the children, and day care, and baby food . . .

Come on Gayle, she chided herself. It's a little silly to get shook up about caring for kids who never existed.

But the underlying question was what was really important. Had loving Craig become just a habit?

The lift creaked to a stop, and she steadied herself. 'You have to do your job this afternoon,' she reminded herself. 'Tonight, after the party, you can dissect the past and find out what you learned.'

In the meantime, it was enough to know that Darrel had been correct, that her days of mourning for Craig were over, that she was free to love again—more wisely next time, and for always.

It felt good, she thought. She'd worn that suit of armour for so long that she hadn't even noticed when it vanished.

Thomas looked up from his post at the information desk. He was in his element today, answering questions for the caterers, the workmen, the string ensemble. Gayle couldn't help being amused, though, at the quiet respect in his voice when he spoke to her these days. The scare Thomas had got when the news of the engagement had swept the building would probably keep him straight for weeks. He was interested in protecting his job, and he was being more careful about confiding his thoughts to his fellow workers.

Gayle looked over the lobby, at the electricians who were checking out the sound system, at the carpenters whose hammers still pounded rhythmically on the last bits of work.

Hard to believe, she thought, that in another few hours all evidence of this work would be gone, and the noise would be the hum of computers and conversation, the clatter of printers and serving trays, the splash of champagne and the fountain.

The caterers had turned the lobby into a sidewalk cafe, surrounding the fountain with small glass-topped tables, each with its own bright umbrella. Around the outer perimeter, under the mezzanine balcony, a crew was carefully setting up the long rows of Logan computers. Each would be operating tonight, showing off the wide range of uses for this new mechanical genius.

Across the lobby Jared was directing the meticulous placement of each machine, as if a half-inch east or west could mean the failure of his dream.

Dreams again, she thought. Here was a man who had struggled for his dreams, and as each one became secure, he had reached for a higher one. A man whose dreams meant magic for other people, too—dreams that were worth any sacrifice to share——

'Oh, my God,' she whispered, and didn't know that she had spoken. Thomas looked up at her, a question in his eyes, but Gayle didn't see him. She saw only Jared.

Her hand was clenched on the edge of the information desk. If it had not locked there she might have fallen. She was dizzy, and weak.

Craig had left her heart so gradually that she had not even bid him goodbye. And just as slowly, Jared Logan had crept in. 'It isn't possible,' she murmured. But she knew, now, what had happened to her.

She had fallen in love all over again, with a man whose heart had never been touched by any woman. If, indeed, he had a heart at all.

CHAPTER NINE

IT can't be real, she told herself. Love doesn't come like this—this single flash of light that blinds and burns and scorches. But as she looked back on the last confusing three weeks, she was forced to admit that it hadn't been so sudden after all. She might have been slow to realise what was going on, but her feelings for Jared had not burst forth in a moment's time. In the last three weeks, there had been all sort of signs—things that could have told her what was happening to her, if she had only been watching!

She remembered the day Elizabeth had come into her office, and the breathless agony she had endured in those few moments before finding out that the woman was his sister-in-law, not his lover. That sudden sensation, like a lift dropping out from under her, had not been shock at the sudden confrontation with a member of his family, as she had thought. It had been relief.

So much for her plans to choose her love more wisely next time, she thought morosely. It had crept up on her before she had a chance to defend herself. What was it Elizabeth had said—something about Logan charm being deadly. Well, Gayle had found that out for herself, too late, and far too well. If only she had not been so arrogantly confident that his charm could not touch her——! The really aggravating thing about it was that Jared hadn't even tried to charm her. He had done it all unconsciously, and he would be horrified to know what he had done.

Well, he wouldn't find out from her, Gayle swore to herself. She suddenly realised that she was still standing beside the information desk, probably looking as if she'd seen a ghost. She loosened her grip on the table, and tried to regain her balance on shaky feet. She was a professional secretary. She would act like one.

Today, she knew, it would take every ounce of self-control she possessed.

The party was an ordeal. She had expected it to be, of course, even before this sudden terrible knowledge had burst upon her. To play out this travesty in front of a few people was one thing; to perform for a crowd of hundreds in the marble lobby was more than she had bargained for. Now, with that awful revelation fresh in her mind, it took grim determination to keep her standing beside Jared, her hand locked in his, greeting his guests with composure.

He's treating me like Underdog, she thought glumly. My leash is a little different, that's all. The padparadschah ring weighed heavily on her finger tonight.

She tried to free her hand once, but his grip tightened, and he whispered into her ear, 'Would you at least try to smile? You look as if I'm holding you hostage here.'

'You are,' she said between clenched teeth. 'Do you suppose you could take it easy on my hand? I think you've broken it.'

He smiled down at her with a loving light in his eyes, and put a casual kiss on her cheek. Gayle heard a wistful sigh from a woman who was standing near her, wishing, no doubt, that it was she who shared the limelight with him. At that moment Gayle would have gladly traded places.

Damn, she thought. I know it's only a show—and he can still melt my heart with that smile.

If you don't want to be kissed, she told herself firmly, why don't you just give him a black eye? Then he'll leave you alone.

She lost herself for a moment in pleasant specula-tion about the scene that would cause. Then she brought herself back to earth. With as many cameras as were present tonignt, someone would be sure to get a picture.

'By the way,' he said, 'I sent the formal announcement to the papers.' He turned to greet another guest.

Gayle was in shock. He can't do that to me, she thought. Surely he's only teasing ...

But Jared didn't tease. She gritted her teeth and tried to resign herself; after all, half of the civilized world already knew about it, so what difference could it make to announce it to the other half? Perhaps it was a good thing after all that Jared had told Darrel about it at lunch today. She could almost hear what Rachel would have had to say if it had glared out at her from the society page tomorrow as she drank her morning coffee.

'I'll take you out for a late supper after the party's over,' Jared said. It wasn't an invitation; it was more like an order.

But Gayle shook her head. 'Thanks, anyway. Tonight, I think I'd rather get some sleep.' She turned her attention to a nearby cluster of guests, and ignored Jared's scowl.

The Glenns came midway through the evening. By then, Jared was demonstrating the new computer himself, showing it off to a group of reporters from the specialty magazines that would, next month, be featuring it. Gayle was nearby, but she was keeping an eye on the caterer's table across the lobby, watching as the waiters replenished the food so smoothly that the trays looked as if they had never been touched. The champagne was flowing in abundance, and the guests were obviously having a good time. Some of them had even started to dance to the Mozart minuets from the string ensemble. So far, she thought, the party was going very smoothly.

She had almost begun to hope that Russell and Krystal Glenn might pass up the evening's entertainment. Perhaps, Gayle thought, Krystal was unhappy about her father's decision to sell Softek—so upset that she had refused to come.

No such luck, Gayle realised when she looked up to see Krystal, in a white velvet cape, coming in. She looked like the snow queen, her blonde hair glowing against the velvet collar. Krystal would never have missed this party, Gayle concluded. She had simply waited to make a grand entrance in front of the greatest number of people.

She fluttered across the room to Jared and almost flung herself into his arms. 'Darling, I'm so proud,' she said, in her little-girl voice. 'Now you must show me everything about this little machine.'

Jared laughed. 'I doubt you need any instruction, Krystal.'

'When I think of the things I could learn from you——'
Krystal sighed dreamily. Her eyes met Gayle's, and for an instant there was a hard, cold challenge in them.

Gayle pretended not to see her. She looked up at Russell Glenn, who had followed quietly in his daughter's wake, with a smile. 'Would you like a glass of champagne, Russell?' she asked calmly, and signalled one of the white-coated waiters.

Out of the corner of her eye, she saw Jared removing Krystal's cape. As if he was undressing a doll, she thought, and was horrified at the stab of pain that shot through her at the very idea. She tried to soothe it by remembering the long line of lovely women in his life, much as she would have tried counting sheep to lull herself to sleep. Krystal would last no longer than any of the others, she told herself.

But their faces had become dim in her mind. They all looked the same anyway, she told herself flatly. They were all beautifully brittle. They were all like plastic dolls, and none of them mattered.

'Every man you date will have a past,' Rachel had pointed out once.

I wouldn't mind his past, Gayle thought painfully. If

I was only sure that I would be his future———!

But as soon as this farce was over, he would go back to them—to the lovely women like Krystal who knew the rules of the game, who sought, as he did, pleasure for tonight without concern for tomorrow.

You did it this time, Gayle, she told herself bitterly. You really set yourself up, and you will be paying for the rest of your life.

A sudden, shocked silence had fallen over the group of reporters—mostly men—who surrounded Jared. Gayle thought it was a little strange, until she saw the gown that Krystal's white velvet cape had concealed.

The dress was a shimmer of silver sequins under the party lights. It hugged Krystal's slender figure and plunged without thought of decency almost to her navel. The back of the dress was nearly non-existent—a few narrow straps lacing it together were the only things that kept it on at all. On Krystal, it looked like a million dollars.

It was an absolutely outrageous dress, totally out of place at a party of this sort. It belonged in a bordello, Gayle thought, and fought down the knowledge that her own moss green chiffon suddenly felt as dowdy as a Puritan's cap and apron.

Krystal glanced around at the shocked faces and pouted prettily, 'Don't you like my new dress, Jared?'

'It's beautiful, Krys,' he said. 'Shall we continue with the demonstration, gentlemen?'

But Gayle saw that his hand lingered at Krystal's waist as he drew her into the group. She wasn't the only one who saw; several of the reporters met her gaze with something like sympathy in their eyes.

They know him very well, Gayle thought.

Then Krystal looked up with a cold smile, her big blue eyes full of wicked triumph as she stared at Gayle. It was a declaration of war.

That dress not only fits like a snakeskin, Gayle thought, a little shaken by the venom in Krystal's eyes, but it's being worn by a snake. A deadly poisonous cobra, at that.

Her lips felt stiff, but she returned Krysal's smile and strolled across to the caterer's table, trying not to run.

Natalie Weston was there. She was in costume tonight, to match the poster-sized ad pictures that were hung around the lobby. She was nibbling lobster patties, and a little earlier, Gayle had noticed that the beauty looked a bit sullen tonight. But she had seen what had happened across the room, and her face had brightened.

'Got a little problem tonight, Gayle?' she drawled, amused. 'You never thought Jared would be so hard to hang on to, did you?'

Gayle knew she shouldn't respond to the catty remark. But before she could bite her tongue, she heard herself saying, 'Did you find that out from experience, Mrs Weston?'

Natile's face tightened into a mask of hatred. Gayle didn't wait for an answer. Her business, she told herself firmly, was to make sure this party ran smoothly. That was all.

The caterer's men were cleaning up the wreckage when she came to work the next day. The carpenters were tearing down the long tables that they had been building all week. The computers were already gone, to be set up in the showroom.

Thomas was at the information desk. He looked almost as tired as Gayle felt. 'The coffee will help,' she told him, nodding towards the cup he held, as she waited for a lift.

He looked stricken. He nodded uncertainly, stared into the cup, and quickly put it down behind the counter.

Gayle reached for it. 'What's in the cup, Thomas?' she asked suspiciously.

'There was a little champagne left over in the bottom of a bottle——' he began nervously.

'And all the fizz is gone by now. Thomas, you must be desperate.'

'It was just a little bit——'

'Get rid of it. And get some coffee in that cup.'

He shuddered artistically. 'I never drink the stuff.'

'You'd better start this morning,' she warned unsympathetically.

'You wouldn't tell the boss, would you, Miss Bradley? After all, he has a bar in his office.'

'I won't tell him about the half inch of champagne, no. He has more important things to think about. But don't do it again.'

Jared was already in the office. He'd been there ahead of her on several days in the past couple of weeks. Gayle thought about commenting on the pleasant effect that clean living was having on his work, but she thought better of it. Besides, she told herself, for all she knew he was still sneaking women into that penthouse apartment every night. Or joining them in their hotel suites——

Oh, stop it, Gayle, she told herself irritably. It's not as if the man is committing adultery, after all. And it is none of your business, no matter what he does.

But, the little devil at the back of her head reminded, he hasn't asked you to send flowers to anyone in three weeks . . .

She flung her handbag into a drawer with unnecessary force and picked up her notebook.

He had propped his feet up and was staring out the wide windows. Thin winter sunlight trickled over Denver itself, and the skyline was shiny in the yellow glow. But off to the west, dark clouds hung low over the foothills.

'It will snow before dark,' Gayle said.

Jared didn't look up. 'That's a pessimist talking,' he mused. 'She looks out at sunshine and predicts snow.'

'Pessimistic, possibly. Experienced in this weather, certainly.'

'And even if it snows,' he added thoughtfully, 'it will just make the skiing conditions better when the whole family gets here in three weeks.'

Gayle straightened the blotter on his desk and picked up a handful of pencils. 'At least by that time the Softek purchase will be completed, and this ridiculous game will be over.'

He didn't answer, just stroked one finger over his moustache. His forehead was lined, as if his thoughts were too harsh to bear.

'It will be over, won't it?' Gayle was beginning to feel a little desperate.

He sighed. 'Probably not,' he said. 'Russ doesn't want to sign the papers until the federal government has decided whether the combination will be unfair competition——'

'That's not very businesslike of him.'

Jared sighed. 'He owns the company, honey. He sets the rules. And I'm sure Krystal had a great deal to say about it.'

'Jared, you told me in the beginning that this would last only a few days. Now you're telling me that it could be weeks more?' Her voice was beginning to rise.

'I didn't expect Russ to stay around Denver,' he said defensively. 'If he and Krystal had gone back to California where they belong——'

'Well, you should expect her to hang around. You've certainly encouraged her!'

'What does that mean?'

Gayle raised her eyes heavenward. 'If you don't know by now, then there is no hope for you at all.' There was a long silence, and then she said, a little panicky, 'Jared—what are we going to do? When your family comes, I mean.'

He raised an eyebrow. 'Go skiing,' he said, as if he was talking to a kindergartner.

'You know what I mean! Aren't you going to tell them the truth?'

'I don't know,' he said finally.

'If you don't,' she threatened, 'I will. It's ridiculous, after all. So much for your wonderful laws of business——'

'It's the first time it ever backfired on me.' He looked puzzled, as if he was trying to play a new game without reading the rules.

'The situation is full of firsts,' Gayle pointed out grimly. 'So why don't we get to work this morning and see if we can speed things along?'

The snowstorm hit at midafternoon. If it hadn't been for the sudden darkness, Gayle would probably not have noticed, for she had her head buried in corporate tax records, trying to distill the information necessary for the government forms. It was hard enough to get the right figures, but what was really complicating the job was that every time she had nearly completed a step, someone came in, or the telephone rang, and she had to start all over.

Once it was the advertising manager. 'Ron,' she told him wearily, 'Jared's desk is swamped. He's trying to stay clear of everything but this application——'

'He can't stay clear of this problem,' Ron said grimly.

She stared at him for a moment, and her professional judgment told her that it was, indeed, important. She reached for the intercom.

'You used to call him Mr Logan,' Ron mused. 'I guess that was why I thought you weren't interested in him. Sorry if I made you uncomfortable, Gayle, but I really do like you.'

She didn't bother to answer. What kind of repsonse was possible, anyway?

Jared sounded just as harried as she felt, but he agreed to see Ron. She waved the ad man into the inner office and started on her column of figures again with a sigh.

The snow swirled down from a leaden sky, and the wind rose slowly, so gradually that it was howling around the building before she noticed. Then she just wearily drew blinds so she didn't have to see it, and went back to work.

By six o'clock, she had made scarcely a dent in the pile of forms. Her intercom buzzer rang, and she swore under her breath as she answered it.

'Gayle, call that little resuaurant down the street——'

And order an intimate supper for two, she supplied mentally. It was the old story all over again. Who, she wondered, would be joining him in the love nest tonight?

'I assume that you can stay late?' he continued.

'I'm still here,' she pointed out. 'And it's already late.'

'Good girl. We'll take a break for supper and keep on working. It should go faster when there is no one in the building to interrupt.'

Clean living, she thought. He'd better be careful; it might get to be a habit.

When the busboy brought up the basket, only his eyes were visible under the snow that caked his scarf and hat.

'It must be quite a storm?' Gayle said, making aimless conversation. She reached for her handbag; anyone who came out in weather like this deserved a nice tip.

'I've seen worse.' His voice was muffled by the heavy scarf wrapped around his face.

She gave him her last five dollars. She had forgotten, in the rush of yesterday's party and today's frantic workload, to go to the bank. There would be no lunch tomorrow until she got some cash, that was certain.

She tapped on Jared's door and took the basket in. 'Dinner is served,' she said.

He tossed his pen down and leaned back in his chair,

stretching. 'And I am starved. Did we take time out for lunch?'

'Now that you mention it—no.' She started to unpack the basket. Curiosity tingled up her spine. She hadn't specified a menu; what did the chef usually send for occasions like this? Of course, she thought. A bottle of champagne would be the first thing. It was even pre-chilled by the outdoor wind.

Nothing had been overlooked. Cloth napkins, silverware—'You must have service for five hundred of the restaurant's china,' she said, taking out two carefully wrapped plates.

Jared shook his head. 'They retrieve the basket the next day.'

'And here I thought you were a genuine big spender.' She opened a foam container. 'It's prime rib tonight. Rare.'

'Good. I could stand a solid chunk of red meat.'

'You would have made a great cave-man. You have all the instincts.'

He ignored the jibe. 'Shall we open the champagne?'

'Not if we plan to get any work done later.'

He raised an eyebrow. 'What would you suggest we do instead of working?'

Gayle fought down a flood of colour that threatened to overwhelm her. 'Shall we stop fencing and just enjoy the food?'

'But it's so much fun to make you blush.'

She hadn't realised just how hungry she was, until she had polished off the blueberry blintze that the chef had thoughtfully provided for deseert. She sat back with a satisfied sigh.

Jared had lighted a cigar and poured a couple of fingers of brandy from the bar in his bookcase. He blew a thoughful smoke ring towards the ceiling. 'Why are you a secretary?' he asked, finally.

'Have you been talking to my brother?' It popped out before she could stop herself.

He looked vaguely interested. 'No. Should I have?'

'It's just that Darrel has a theory about everything,' she said, trying to minimise her mistake. 'I told you once—I'm darn good at carrying out decisions, but I don't want to be the one to make them. I'm a very good follower, and I'd rather stay in the background.'

There was a long, thoughtful pause as Jared studied the glowing ash of his cigar. 'Well, whatever the reason,' he drawled finally, 'I'm not fool enough to give you a promotion.'

Gayle didn't argue. She didn't care what he thought of her reasons, she told herself firmly. 'And you? Why computers?'

For a moment she thought that he hadn't heard her. Then he looked up. 'I almost didn't, you know,' he said. 'My father wasn't impressed by what he called my childish attachment to a silly hobby—and there was a soft job waiting for me with his banks. It was tempting.' Then he smiled, 'No—not soft, exactly. There's no such thing as an easy job with the Logan Banks.'

'It must be convenient to have a banker in the family.'

'Don't bet on it. There are much easier people to get loans from than Whit Logan—which explains why Logan bank stock is sky-high when other financial institutions are going broke.'

'And now he's your biggest customer,' Gayle said softly.

Jared smiled. 'That's right. He finally had to admit that my juvenile passion, combined with all the ins and outs of banking that he'd taught me over the years, could be a giant leap forward for his business.'

'You sound very fond of him.'

'Grady and I learned early that no one else had a father like ours. He's an overbearing autocrat, and sometimes he doesn't know how to mind his own business——' He looked up with a boyish smile. 'But yes, I do kind of like the old guy.'

'It's an unusual family,' Gayle mused. 'Christmas in New York——'

'And Labor Day on Lake Michigan. And a week in March on the ski slopes.' He yawned. 'And that's only the official get-togethers.'

How pleasant it would be to be part of such a family, she thought. But there was no sense in thinking about it, she told herself firmly. She glanced at the clock. 'Time to go back to work,' she said.

'The heck with it. We can't finish tonight anyway. I'll take you home.'

She had to admit that home—her own snug little living room—sounded good. She'd already put in such long hours in the office this week that she was beginning to think she'd moved in.

'I can just call a cab,' she said.

He shook his head. 'Get your coat.'

The wind blasting down the canyons formed by skyscrapers sucked the oxygen from Gayle's lungs the instant they stepped outside the door. The snow was now mixed with sleet, and the sharp particles felt like tiny knives slicing her skin. She pulled the scarf up over her cheeks. 'It's wicked out here!' she called.

Jared nodded. He was hatless, and the snow was already settling on his dark hair in a crust. 'It's two blocks down to the car,' he warned.

'I've walked in worse. It feels as if we're in a paperweight,' she said brightly. 'You know—those glass ones with the miniature scenes and the snowstorm inside when they're shaken.'

He grunted. 'Yeah, maybe it's all a joke.'

Once around the corner of the building, Gayle realised that she had never seen anything like this. The howling wind whipped the snow into a fog, and sometimes she could see just a few feet. Her breath was coming hard before they had walked the first block, and if it hadn't been for Jared's hand firmly on her arm, she would have fallen more than once.

He swore, and pushed her gently into the doorway of a building. No wind could penetrate the little nook, but the air was still frigid.

'I'm sorry,' she said. 'It was a little foolish to leave my snowboots at home today——'

He cut her off abruptly. 'It isn't that. Haven't you noticed that there is not a single vehicle on the streets? This is a main route—there should be a couple of ploughs running right here.'

'Maybe they're just out of sight——' she ventured.

Jared ran his gloved fingers through his hair, and a tiny snowstorm fell out. 'They've been pulled off the streets,' he said flatly. 'I'm in no mood to take the Jaguar out in this.'

'I'd hate to be the cause of a bent-up fender,' Gayle agreed.

'I'm not afraid of banging up the car. But if I'm going to be stranded, I'd much rather it be in a warm building than out on the streets. Let's get our breath and go back.'

It seemed impossible that the storm had worsened in the brief time they had been sheltered by the doorway. But Gayle was panting by the time they reached the Logan building again. 'I'll call a cab from the office,' she said.

He didn't bother to answer. In the mirrored lift, she was shocked by the snow that had caked into the folds of her scarf. Ice crystals had frozen on her eyelashes, and as they began to melt she felt as if she were mopping tears.

'You shouldn't go out without a hat,' she said, and reached up to brush snow out of his hair.

He caught her hand, and the padparadschah ring flared even in the dim light of the elevator. For a long moment she looked up into his eyes, and wondered dizzily if he could see into her thoughts and know how much she loved him.

Then he released her hand, and said, 'You'll get frostbite, playing in the snow without your gloves.'

Relieved, she turned towards the door as it opened, and then stood as if the chill had frozen her solid. For it was not the executive office suite she was looking at, but the penthouse floor.

He had brought her to the love nest.

CHAPTER TEN

DON'T be ridiculous, she told herself firmly. Of course he brought you here. The only alternative would be to sleep on a desk down in the office. At least here there is a bedroom——

One bedroom, she remembered that Elizabeth had said.

Dammit, Gayle, she ordered herself, grow up! After all, a night at the love nest with her hadn't exactly been in Jared's plans, any more than it had been in hers. He'd made a frantic effort to get her home. The least she could do would be to accept his forced hospitality with graciousness, and not start getting hysterical.

But she couldn't help looking at the double doors of the apartment, carved from heavy walnut, with forebodding.

He unlocked the doors and pushed them open. 'We'd better get you dried off,' he said impersonally. 'I can't afford to have you down with pneumonia.'

In those brief minutes of exposure to the storm, the snow had driven through her scarf, under the hem of her coat, up her sleeves. As the crystals began to melt, the cuffs and skirt of her dress grew soggy. Gayle squirmed out of her coat and sneaked a cautious look around.

So this was the fabled love nest, she thought.

A grey brick wall greeted her, separating the entryway from the living room which must lay beyond. The wall was at least twenty feet long, an unbroken expanse of irregular shapes which formed a sculptural pattern all its own. To her left were two shallow steps leading down into the living room. All she could see of the room was a concert grand piano and the bank of windows that now looked out at the driving snow.

Jared hung her coat up and said, 'I think a hot shower is the best thing for you.' He led the way down the shallows steps.

Gayle stopped in the centre of the living room. She didn't know quite what she had expected. Lamps shaped like bare-breasted hula girls, perhaps—or chairs upholstered in zebra skins,. Instead, like Pino Reposo, the penthouse was simple, understated, elegant. On the living room side of the grey brick wall was the biggest fireplace Gayle had ever seen. In front of it was a long, semicircular couch upholstered in grey leather. It could probably seat a dozen people, and it was nestled into a conversation pit two steps lower than the rest of the room. The only other furniture in the enormous living room was the piano and a wall of cabinets that displayed a wet bar, an elaborate stereo system, and hundreds of record albums and tapes behind glass doors. The room glowed under soft, indirect lighting.

An echoing tomb, Elizabeth had called the apartment. It was hardly that, Gayle thought, but it was stark and sparsely furnished. The only ornament was a bronze statue on a pedestal near the huge windows. It was a cowboy riding a bucking horse, and if it wasn't an original Frederic Remington, then the artist himself probably couldn't have told the difference, she decided.

Her fingers itched to add some personal touches—a Norfolk pine tree in a pot near the windows. Some big cushions to be dragged around and sat on. An Oriental porcelain here and there. A fern to soften the outline of the huge piano . . . What was Jared doing with a concert grand, anyway, she wondered idly.

He was waiting for her across the room, arms folded, impatience beginning to write itself on his face. She remembered abruptly that she was staring, and followed him, her feet sinking into the deep grey-blue carpet. It was the perfect room for kicking off one's shoes, she thought.

'It sort of took me by surprise,' she said, with a note of apology in her voice.

He didn't comment, just pushed open another door. This one was the bedroom, she saw. The enormous bed had a masculine version of a canopy—a starkly simple dark mahogany frame.

'The bathroom is through there,' Jared said. 'I'll hunt you out something to wear—but I make no promises on how it will fit.'

She might have agrued, but her dress was uncomfortably wet by now, and she was beginning to feel chilled. So she tried to laugh the problem away. 'Hasn't a lady ever mistakenly left her black lace negligée behind?'

'No,' he said shortly. 'And if one had, I wouldn't recommend that you wear it.'

Gayle bit her lip. So much for that joke, she thought wearily. Well, he was right—she wasn't exactly the black lace negligée type.

'Look,' she said. 'I'm really sorry you have to put up with me——'

'Don't fret about it. Just go get into the shower. Or soak in the whirlpool if you like—it takes a while to fill, but it's well worth the wait.' He was rummaging through drawers that had been concealed by a mirrored door.

'What about you? You're all wet too.' Then she flushed scarlet and hoped that he wouldn't think she was issuing an invitation to join her.

He didn't bother to answer, so Gayle went on into the bathroom. She was so startled by it that she allowed herself a tuneless little whistle. This has to be the most sinfully luxurious bathroom in Denver, she thought. For starters, it was bigger than the bedroom, and the centre of attention was a whirlpool tub large enough for four people. The taps were gold, she'd bet her life, and above the tub was a low mirrored ceiling surrounded by soft spot lights.

'This is the kind of thing that led to the fall of the Roman empire,' Gayle muttered. She walked resolutely past the hot tub, trying to ignore the little voice that urged her to try it out. 'A shower will be perfectly good enough,' she told herself firmly.

The water in the shower was hot, and she stood letting the needle spray massage the tense muscles in her back. 'Maybe I can just stand here all night,' she murmured. But eventually she forced herself to turn the water off. Jared might want a shower, too. It wasn't fair of her to monopolise the bathroom.

Here, too, was a mirrored wall that concealed closets. 'Plenty of places for the lovelies to admire themselves,' Gayle muttered. She found a big bathsheet and fashioned it into a toga. She dried off her hair under the heat lamp and left it in a mass of tangled curls. Who cared, anyway? she thought. Jared certainly wouldn't.

She was back in the bedroom before it occurred to her that he might still be there. But there was only silence. A robe and a pair of red silk pyjamas were laid out on the foot of the bed,.

She touched the pyjama jacket with a tentative finger, hardly believing it was real. Surely no one actually wore this kind of thing, she thought. But Jared's initials were monogrammed on the pocket.

She fought off the giggles and put the jacket on, rolling the sleeves up to free her hands. The trousers, even with a drawstring waist, were too big, and she reluctantly put them aside. The blue velvet robe was also his, and she felt like a midget as she tucked it up with the tie belt so she wouldn't trip over the hem.

Then she took a deep breath and started down the hall. The apartment was quiet, except for the ripple of a piano sonata. Beethoven's *Pathetique*, she thought. So there were some classical things in that phenomenally large collection of records, were there? A girl could find out a lot about Jared Logan here, if she wanted to try.

She rounded the corner into the living room on silent feet, her hands tucked into the gigantic pockets of the robe. She felt like a Shakespearean heroine sweeping on to a stage.

Then she saw Jared at the piano, his fingers flying through the allegro first movement of the *Pathetique*. He was so absorbed in the music that he hadn't seen her come in.

She drew back instinctively into the hallway, feeling as though she had trespassed inexcusably on a moment so purely personal that no one should ever share it. She hovered there, listening intently. He stumbled once, played the passage through very slowly, then attacked it again. She found herself smiling as the movement closed, the triumphant final bars vibrating through the room.

I'll bet he doesn't do that for every woman who comes here, she thought. And then answered herself— Of course not. Usually he's too busy entertaining them in other ways.

She waited till the small noises told her he was at the bar. Then she picked up the trailing hem of the robe and went in.

He was working a cork from a champagne bottle. It gave a satisfying pop, and he poured a bit into a glass and tasted it. 'Out of the shower already?' he asked, handing her a tulip-shaped glass.

'I thought you'd want one.' She sipped the wine. He'd changed clothes, she saw, to a ski sweater and casual slacks. She felt a little underdressed.

'Later.'

'What's the occasion?' she asked, gesturing with the glass.

'Haven't you been listening to the wine sellers? On a special day, any wine will do. But if it isn't an occasion, champagne makes it one .   . Cheers.'

'Whatever you say.' He'd built a fire, and she strolled down into the conversation pit to sit in front of it. The flames popped and sparked against the glass doors, and heat radiated out towards her bare toes. 'Actually, we should be thinking positive about this whole thing,' she said. 'If the snow keeps up, nobody else will get to the office tomorrow. With the place to ourselves, we can finish up those applications in record time.'

'I wouldn't bet on it. We'll get to do all their work too. I was thinking about it—let's just go up to Pino Reposo this weekend, take the 'phone off the hook, tell Peters to keep Underdog out of our hair, and work till it's done.'

Another weekend at Pino Reposo? Knowing as she now did that she would love him forever, could she bear to do that?

'I can't,' she said. 'I promised Darrel I'd take care of his little girl this weekend.'

He frowned. 'How little?'

'Three.'

'I guess that eliminates working the weekend, doesn't it? Want something to snack on? I found caviar and crackers.'

'I'll pass.' She fought off a whisper of disappointment—now, she would probably never see Pino Reposo again. Then, curiously, she asked, 'Caviar and crackers? Don't you ever do anything the sane way, Jared?'

He shrugged and came to sit beside her. 'Of course not. It's no fun. How did the pyjamas fit?'

'Very badly. I would have had to roll up half of the legs, so I left the trousers for you.' Her voice was sweet.

He ran an appraising eye over her figure, swathed in the velvet robe. 'If we get an invitation to a come-as-you-are party, I'll turn it down.'

'Thanks. I must admit, I didn't expect red silk pyjamas. Do you have a whole drawer of them, in rainbow colours?'

'As a matter of fact, they were a Christmas gift, and you are the first to wear them.'

Gayle didn't think she wanted to pursue that line of thought any further. He set his champagne glass on the ledge that circled the couch. The glass was right behind her head, and his fingers brushed lightly over her hair. She tried to ignore him. 'Shall we put on some music?' she asked. 'I'm dying to look through your albums.'

'What kind?' His fingers played over a little control panel that was built into the ledge. The lights dimmed gradually.

'Classical.'

He pushed another button, and the soft strains of Tchaikovsky filled the room.

'NOT *Romeo and Juliet*,' Gayle said, and jumped up.

'Very good,' he said. 'Not many people can recognise that one in two measures. Shall we have a drop-the-needle challenge? I'll play one minute at random from a piece of music, and if you can't identify it——'

'I don't think so,' Gayle said. She was looking through the albums. Anything non-romantic would do, she thought, and settled on the *1812 Overture*.

He raised an eyebrow. 'Well, we must find some way to entertain ourselves till bedtime.'

She put the record on, and came back to sit a safe distance from him. 'Chicken,' he said softly. 'Are you ready for your kissing exam?'

She didn't answer. He laughed, put another log on the fire, and refilled their champagne glasses. Then he sat down beside her.

It was the first time she had ever been kissed with martial music in the background, and Gayle had to admit hazily after a moment that it wouldn't have mattered a darn if there'd been an entire high school band playing *The Star-Spangled Banner* directly into her left ear. She would still have dissolved in Jared's arms, helpless to resist that consummate charm.

'Much better,' he said, raising his head. 'You're a fast learner.'

And that's precisely what it means to him, she thought. It wasn't fair! Her blood pressure was sky-high, but he wasn't even ruffled.

She picked up her glass and tried to pretend that it was a shield. 'You never did answer my question tonight,' she said, trying to suppress the breathlessness in her voice.

He traced a gentle path down the side of her face with a fingertip. 'Which question?' he asked huskily?

'Why computers? You never told me what the fascination is.'

He smiled, slowly. 'You know that you don't really want to talk about computers.'

'Yes, I do.' There was a hint of panic in her voice. If I don't get this conversation back on a calmer note, she thought, I am going to end up throwing myself at him—and I'll be so thorougly embarrassed that I will never recover.

She had been foolish enough to think that the stunning realisation of her love would make it easier to deal with him. She loved him, and the fact that he didn't love her should have kept her safe. If she just kept telling herself that he was only toying with her affections because he was bored, that he was nothing more than a playboy . . .

But it wasn't working. When she was close to him, the only thing she could remember was that she loved him. Nothing else mattered at all.

He stretched out, one arm casually around her. He drew her head down on to his shoulder, and his breath stirred her hair. 'This is nice,' he said. 'It could get to be a habit.'

She stayed very quiet, trying not to breathe.

'Computers,' he mused. 'Funny you should ask that. I've never really thought about it—they were just always there.'

The soft wool of his sweater was tickling her nose, but she didn't want to move, to shatter this magic moment.

'It's the pure logic, I suppose,' he mused. 'To a computer, everything has to be either yes or no—on or off. There is nothing in between—no maybes or somewhats or possiblies. It's such a tidy way to organise life.'

'But it's so artificial,' she objected.

'Yes. That's the challenge of programming—to reduce all the infinite possibilites to a series of yes or no questions. To eliminate all the maybes, so that the computer can mimic the real thing.'

She thought about that one for a minute. 'Is that why you want Softek so much?'

'Not entirely. I could expand the programming division we have now. I'm going to do that anyway, by the way. We'll be starting a new line of computer games aimed at adults instead of kids. More sophisticated subjects——'

'Those kids are pretty sophisticated already,' she objected.

'I know. I've been working on a couple of games ideas, and they're unbelievably difficult to program.' There was a long silence, as if he was thinking about it. 'But I still want Softek. All really new ideas come from small companies, and it has a reputation——' His voice trailed off.

'Would you have married Krystal Glenn?' Her voice was low. The hypnotic effect of the fire and the warm, dim room were making her sleepy. The *Overture* had long since played itself out, and the only sound was the hiss of the embers in the fireplace and the strong beat of his heart against her ear.

'I thought I told you that I don't believe in marriage.'

'That doesn't answer my question.'

'A half-grown, spoiled child?'

'But she's lovely,' Gayle said softly.

'Sure, she's lovely. So are a lot of other women. And they will not—unlike Krystal—turn into domineering shrews in ten years.'

Gayle could imagine what the woman would be like. 'And you wouldn't have married her?' she quizzed softly. 'Not even to get what you want?'

'No, Gayle. There are limits, and I draw the line at marriage.' He rubbed his chin against the top of her head.

She twisted around on the couch, trying to get more comfortable, and then sat up. 'Psychologists have a theory about men like you, you know.'

'Oh, really?' A smile tugged at the corner of his mouth.

'Yes. They say that a man with a Don Juan fixation refuses to get involved because he is afraid that once a woman knows him well, she'll find out about all of his shortcomings.'

He shrugged. 'Nobody's perfect.'

'And she might reject him,' Gayle continued. 'So to prevent that from happening, he rejects her before she has the chance to find out all about him.'

He said, his voice dry, 'Is that the total of this new revelation, or is there more?'

'That's one school of thought. On the other hand,' Gayle added brightly, 'another group of psychologists feel that womanisers may just be going through delayed adolescence.'

He made a grab for her, and missed. 'You little——'

She had bounded off the couch and up the steps to the main part of the living room. 'Your interest in the new line of adult games would seem to back up the second theory,' she pointed out.

'When I catch you,' he threatened, 'I'll show you adult games!'

She laughed at him, certain that he wasn't serious. In any case, she could elude him easily.

But it didn't quite work that way. He moved faster

than she had figured on, and she had forgotten about the long hem of her robe. She tripped over it just as he reached for her, and the two of them hit the carpet at the same instant.

'Are you all right?' he asked.

Gayle nodded. His midnight blue eyes were just inches away. She could have counted his eyelashes, she thought muzzily, if only she hadn't been so breathless that she couldn't remember how to count . . .

His mouth was fiery, demanding possessive. He seemed to absorb all her strength, leaving her clinging to him, trembling. There was a light of triumph in his eyes as he raised his head, and a long shiver ran through Gayle. My God, she thought, he knows he's won . . .

The velvet robe had twisted around her when she fell, loosening the belt. Jared slowly untied it and spread the velvet out around her. She had no will power left to resist.

The pyjama jacket had pulled taut across her breasts, and he smiled as he traced the outline of his initials on the monogrammed pocket. To Gayle, it felt as if she was being branded. The thin silk could not conceal the eager nipple, and the barest pressure of his fingers sent chills over her, brought her breath fast and painful, aroused every nerve until her whole body was screaming.

'You promised that you wouldn't seduce me,' she whispered. Her voice cracked.

'For your information, honey,' he said, very softly, 'you're the one who started this, with your little psychologist number.' His lips traced slowly down her throat to the shadow between her breasts, and his fingers toyed with the top button.

She clenched her fists and fought the sensation. She struggled against the temptation to give in, to pull him down to her, to share with him that fullness of love as she longed to do . . .

She let her body go limp, and when he stopped nibbling at her throat and raised a questioning eyebrow, she said, 'What about music?'

The eyebrow went even higher. 'If you'd like, I'll put something on. But frankly, I thought we were doing very well without it.'

'Not the albums,' she said. She was having trouble shaping the words. 'If your attraction to computers is perfect logic, how do you account for the music?'

'Simple,' he murmured. 'Every woman's taste is different——'

'I mean the *Pathetique*, Jared. You don't pick that up overnight.'

'Ah,' he said mildly. 'You were eavesdropping. Could we discuss this some other time?'

'I was listening from the hallway,' she admitted. 'It was beautiful. Will you play it again?'

'Look, I'm really delighted to know that Beethoven turns you on. But since I can only use my hands to do one thing at a time, could you possibly wait till tomorrow for the concert?'

'I mean it, Jared. It's obvious that the piano is a passion——' She was breathing a little more easily now, and her mind was functioning more clearly.

'There are all sort of passions, Gayle. But if you insist on discussing music, I suppose it was the logical progression that drew me into it. Music is just audible mathematics, after all. Neat little symmetrical patterns. Now can we——'

'I thought the two things must have something in common. And then we come to women—it's purely numbers, there, too, isn't it, Jared?'

He sighed. 'Do you really want me to stop kissing you?'

'Yes.' She pushed him away gently.

'Liar,' he said, very softly.

She didn't intend to be drawn into an argument about it. 'Why don't you show me the new games you're working on?'

'Sure you want to see them?'

'I'll be your first test-market.'

An amused smile played over his face. 'Positive, Gayle?'

She should have been warned. But at that moment she would have done anything, she said anything in order to get up from the carpet, away from the danger that his mere presence created for her. 'You never believe anything I say.'

'That's because most of the time you don't mean it.' He pulled her to her feet. 'To the bedroom, my dear.'

'Wait a minute. You said adult sophistication—not X-rated.'

'See? You're already backing out. I've been thinking of doing strip poker—but the computer wouldn't cheat, and that's half the fun.' He gave her a lecherous grin, and them sobered. 'Actually, the only television set is in the bedroom, and the computer is hooked up to it. Cross my heart and hope to die, I have no designs on your virtue.'

'I think I've heard that line before,' Gayle said tartly. In for a penny, she thought. She followed him meekly down the hall and sat stiffly on the corner of the bed.

He sprawled across the quilt and opened a drawer in the built-in nightstand. Inside it was a row of buttons, and he pushed one. Across the room, a big chest silently opened and a huge television screen rose to dominate the room. He tossed her a control stick. 'You are about to be the first person to get wiped out at this game, Gayle,' he warned.

'I'll take my chances.' It took a few minutes to catch on, but soon she was piling up points. 'This is great,' she said finally. 'Do you realise that with your abilities, you could be the world's best electronic thief?'

'I know,' he said modestly. 'You'd do better if you were comfortable.'

'I'm quite all right,' Gayle assured him stiffly.

Jared just grinned and pulled the quilt back. He piled

the pillows up, leaned back against them, and
proceeded to clear the game board. 'See what I mean?'
he said.

He did look comfortable, and the pile of satin-
covered pillows was inviting. Gayle waited till he was
absorbed in the next round, and crept up to the head
of the bed beside him.

He glanced away from the screen for a moment to
give her a sideways smile.

'You know,' she said when he'd gone down to noble
defeat, 'this must be the most unusual night this
bedroom has ever seen. Really, Jared—I thought that
satin sheets were only legend.'

'Sleep on them once and you'll never go back to
cotton ones,' he said.

'Do all of your guests like them?'

'Why? They're a fact, aren't they? I hope you keep
records—after all, they are the world's most beautiful
women.'

'Most of them didn't have legs as nice as yours.' It
was offhand, matter-of-fact. He was absorbed in the
game.

You asked for that one, Gayle, she told herself. Tease
him about his women, and he will get even. She
laughed. 'If you can't think of a better line than
that——'

'Of course,' he added, 'I didn't see most of them
displayed under quite these circumstances.'

She realised abruptly that the robe had pulled apart,
leaving almost the entire length of her legs bare. She
coloured and rearranged the robe with great care.

Jared shook his head. 'Don't do that. Why be
ashamed of a very nice physical feature? You should
learn how to take a compliment, Gayle.'

'That wasn't a compliment.'

'Yes, it was.' He lost his round, and tossed the
control stick aside. Before she had an inkling of what he
intended, he had seized her ankle. 'Look at this.'

'So? It's an ankle.'

He looked down at her, one eyebrow crooked. 'And a very nicely shaped one, too.' His hand slid, very slowly, up over her calf, her knee, pushing the velvet robe aside. 'Now you say, Thank you, Jared ...' he prompted.

'Are you serious?'

'Very.' His hand crept a little farther up her leg.

'Then——' She looked up into blue eyes dark with intensity. It was hard to frame the words. 'Thank you, Jared.' It was something to treasure, she thought. Whether he really meant it or not, he had said it, and that was something precious.

His hand was resting on the curve of her hip. Then, very slowly, he reached for the buttons on the pyjama jacket.

'You're losing all the points you'd built up,' she murmured.

'They're being sacrificed in a good cause.'

'You said you wouldn't——'

'I lied.' He sounded just a little breathless, she thought. 'I know I warned you about the black lace negliée, but I didn't know myself how sexy a man's pyjamas could be!' His hands were warm through the silk.

'Who give you the pyjamas?' Gayle asked. Her voice was unsteady.

For a moment he seemed not to have heard. 'Elizabeth,' he said finally. 'She told me that every man of the world should own a pair of red silk pyjamas. Now I finally know why. Remind me to call and tell her thanks ...' His voice trailed off as the last button yielded, and he bent his head to nibble at her breast.

I'm glad it was her, Gayle thought, and admitted to herself for the first time just how desperately she wanted him to make love to her.

I need him, she thought. To have him close to me—to

know that there is no other woman at this moment, that for this instant of time he belongs to me——

Then he sighed, and ruffled her hair, and pulled away, his fingers lingering along the swell of her breast. 'Good night, Gayle,' he said, very quietly. 'Sleep well.'

Then he was gone.

She was stunned. Surely this should not have happened. Surely——

Somehow, he knew, she thought. He read me like a book, and he knew that if he made love to me tonight that I could never be like those other women, the ones who play by the rules. And he would never be foolish enough to lose his secretary, he had said. So, rather than mess up his office routine, he had left her there alone.

She punched her pillow up into a wad, taking out a bit of her frustration on the satin case, and turned out the lights.

He was right, she thought wearily. There was something incredibly sexy about sleeping in a man's pyjamas. But at that moment, she would have given anything to have, not the red silk pyjamas, but Jared himself beside her.

And she wondered, with her last conscious thought; If he had stayed with me tonight, would he have sent me roses in the morning?

CHAPTER ELEVEN

GAYLE was still in her robe on Saturday morning, drinking her first cup of coffee and listening to Amy's delighted chatter as the child ate toast and cereal and planned out her day. But much as she loved the dark-haired toddler, Gayle wasn't paying much attention to her conversation.

She was still thinking about the day before. She had scarcely got downstairs to her office before the first smirks had appeared, and it hadn't taken long for the news to spread. By ten o'clock it was obvious that every employee who had struggled in to work that day knew that Gayle had spent the night in the love nest. By eleven, the telephone lines had been humming as they relayed the news to their snowbound co-workers.

Some of them, Gayle thought bitterly, had probably been collecting on bets! And all of them had been astonished that it had taken so long for her to give in and spend the night with Jared . . .

And if they knew what had really happened, they'd be hard pressed to keep from laughing, she thought.

It still smarted, that she had been the one to toss common sense to the winds. 'I should have slapped his face,' she muttered, and poured herself more coffee. 'I should have told him to keep his hands off me——' But she hadn't, and a whole day later, she was still deeply ashamed that Jared had been the only one to exert any self-control.

Amy slid down from her chair, leaving the wreckage of breakfast to be cleaned up.

'What shall we do today?' Gayle asked her.

Amy's big brown eyes glowed. 'The zoo!'

'It's awfully cold and snowy,' Gayle warned. 'The

154

animals won't be coming out to play.' The streets she could see from her apartment looked clear. But as soon as the snowstorm had eased yesterday, the cold had settled in again—the bone-chilling wind that cut through clothes and flesh. She wasn't looking forward to going out in it at all—much less to walk from one end of the zoo to the other in search of a few animals.

She was a little envious of Darrel and Rachel. She'd give anything right now for a bit of the Arizona sunshine they were enjoying.

When they had dropped Amy off last night, they had looked almost like honeymooners. They had been in Rachel's eyes a bit of the glow from her wedding day. Gayle was a little jealous of that, too.

Rachel had swept in like a whirlwind, delighted at the news of Gayle's engagement. She had asked so many questions so fast that there had been no room for answers, which was just as well, as far as Gayle was concerned. She could not have lied to Rachel, and she wasn't sure she wanted to tell the truth, either. So she had forced a smile. Fortunately, Rachel hadn't paused for breath, or she would have realised that the smile was not an appropriate one for a contented bride-to-be.

Gayle knew that she would have to face the questions sooner or later. But for right now, she needed a little time to organise her story and to school her wayward emotions, so that she could make herself—and everyone else—believe that she was all right.

'It was bad enough to fall in love with him,' she told herself morosely. 'But if the world finds out——'

'Why are you talking to yourself?' Amy asked.

Gayle was a bit startled. She'd almost forgotten the child was there. 'Because I'm in the habit. I don't have a little girl to talk to most of the time.'

Amy chewed that one for a few minutes. 'Why don't you get a Daddy and a little girl, like Mommy did?' she asked politely.

'If it were only so easy, Amy.' Not you, too, Gayle

thought. Three years of age was a bit young to start matchmaking. 'I put your clothes out on your bed, dear.'

Amy sighed, a surprisingly mature sound from one so tiny. 'Very well,' she said, and Gayle wondered idly where she'd picked up that expression.

Gayle wandered into the living room, her coffee cup in hand, and stopped beside the mantel. The photograph of Craig on their mountain picnic was still there, and she picked it up, willing herself to feel again the joy of their love. Perhaps this whole episode with Jared was imaginary, she told herself. Perhaps she had only talked herself into love, and if so she could talk herself back out of it.

She stared into the picture, trying to remember the girl she had been. She would even have welcomed the familiar wave of pain; it would have come as a relief. But the whole memory was like a silent movie, running at the wrong speed. She felt only a bit of nostalgia, for a time long past.

The doorbell rang, and Gayle jumped. She wasn't expecting anyone this morning——

Certainly she hadn't prepared herself for the person she saw through the peephole. If she had needed confirmation of her own crazy emotions, her heart gave it to her then. Only one person could make her feel this way.

'You wouldn't happen to have a cup of coffee to spare?' Jared asked when she opened the door.

'Of course.' She looked once more at the photograph in her hand, and then set it down on the coffee table.

Jared glanced at it, and his jaw tightened. 'Have you taken to carrying him around with you now?' he asked.

'What is this, an inquisition?' She led him to the kitchen and handed him a mug.

Jared filled it and glanced around with a raised eyebrow. 'Do you always shred your toast all over the table like that?'

'What? Oh, that was Amy's breakfast.' She wiped up the mess and put it down the garbage disposal.

'I came over hoping to meet this little person. She seems to be the only one in the world who can interfere with your work.' But his tone was teasing.

'She's getting dressed. I'm truly sorry about the weekend, Jared, but——'

'When are we going to get the paperwork done?'

'I'll stay till it's finished Monday. That's a promise.'

He didn't seem to be listening. 'Nice robe,' he said, studying her. 'Fits you much better than mine did.'

Gayle refilled her coffee mug. She was careful not to look at him as she said, 'Did you come here to talk about business or my clothes?'

'Which would be more fun?'

Amy had paused in the doorway, her eyes round as she inspected the newcomer. Then she skirted him slowly and came to Gayle, who set her on the counter to tie her shoes and button her sweater.

'Who's that man?' Amy asked, pointing a finger.

'My name is Jared,' he said, offering her a solemn handshake.

She looked thoughtful. 'Uncle Jared?' she asked.

'That's what your mother told you, yes,' Gayle admitted.

'Do you have any little girls?' Amy asked him.

Gayle put the child down. 'No. Uncle Jared specialises in big girls.'

'That was low,' he complained. 'Have you two made elaborate plans for the weekend?'

'No. Why?'

'Let's take the kid up to Pino Reposo. I don't know why I didn't think of it before. Peters can entertain her.'

'You're anxious to have the papers done.' The sooner those govenment applications were filed she reminded herself, the quicker the sale would be completed, and the sooner this ill-fated engagement would be over. She ought to be delighted at the idea. And yet——

I'm crazy to even think of going up there, she told herself. After what happened at the love nest, I should never be alone with him anywhere except the office. Even in the office, I'm not sure I can always trust myself——

Pino Reposo. The sound of the fountain's trickle seemed to echo in her ears. He had said once that he never took a woman to Pino Reposo . . .

'I'll go pack,' she heard herself saying, very softly.

By the time the Jaguar slowed for the little town near Pino Reposo, Gayle was a bundle of nerves. She said, finally, 'Did you call Peters?'

'Of course,' he said, with a grin. 'I called him right before I came to your apartment, and told him there would be three for lunch.'

'Certain of yourself, aren't you?' Gayle said drily. 'Did you also tell him that one of the three eats only yoghurt and peanut butter? Not at the same time, of course.'

'I didn't know it.'

'In that case, you'd better stop at a store so I can stock up.'

'How much yoghurt can one child eat in two days?'

'You'd be astounded.' She reached for her wallet to check her financial situation, and only then remembered the busboy who had got her last five dollars the night of the storm. She had nothing but a handful of change to her name at the moment; her Denver bank account was not much good when she was a hundred miles away. 'Could you loan me some money?' she asked, feeling like a fool.

'Doesn't your boss pay you well enough?' he teased.

'He didn't pay me back the tip I gave the busboy. And I didn't get to the bank——'

Jared grinned. 'I think I could scrape up a little cash,' he agreed. 'Will a couple of hundred do it?'

'I think I could manage on that for the weekend,' she said primly.

The little general store was like something frozen in time. The products on the shelves were modern, but the atmosphere, the service, the surrounding were of the era when silver mines pumped riches into the town's economy. Gayle picked up the food, then added a colouring book, crayons, and a package of modelling clay. When Jared raised an eyebrow, she said. 'It keeps her entertained for hours.'

He shrugged and turned his attention back to the latest issue of the news magazine that he'd picked up from the counter. It was a bit of a balancing act because he was holding Amy; she had snuggled her head sleepily into his shoulder.

'I'm finished. Would you stop reading the magazines in the store, Jared? It isn't polite.' Then Gayle saw the column he was reading, and her own name leaped out at her.

'You said you sent it to the newspapers,' she snapped. 'But the magazines, too? Jared, for heaven's sake——'

He was shaking his head. She took the hint and waited till they were back in the car. 'I didn't,' he said. 'The news would have spread, of course, but there hasn't been time for the magazines to pick it up.' He tapped the magazine cover. 'This, my dear, is your friend Elizabeth at work. I'd bet on it.'

'Whose side is she on, anyway?' Gayle sputtered. Then, when she saw the lively curiosity in his eyes, she bit her tongue, hard. 'I'd like to just crawl into a cave,' she wailed. 'Jared, isn't there something we can do? This could drag on for months—It's destroying me!'

The car stopped in front of Pino Reposo, Jared unbelted Amy from the back and set her on to the tiled terrace. Then he walked around the car to open Gayle's door.

She was fighting tears. 'Do you have any idea how

difficult it is . . .?' To love you, she thought. To be so close to you, and to wonder what it would be like to have you love me——

He leaned into the car and brushed a hand across her hair. 'I understand, Gayle,' he said. 'I know how hard it is to be patient. I promise you—it will be over soon.'

There was a hard certainty in his voice, a sureness born of disillusionment. It did nothing to relieve her misery.

The weekend, despite the paperwork, was an all-too brief island of peacefulness. Amy played in the courtyard, delighted in this stolen bit of summer, romped with Underdog, and slept with the innocent exhaustion of childhood, unaware of the currents that flowed around her.

Gayle watched the child sleep at night, envious of Amy's ability to forget the cares of the world. She herself had lost track of how many hours she had lain, unable to close her eyes.

Soon it would be over, Jared had said. She didn't doubt his word, though she had no idea how he intended to accomplish it. There was no way to hurry the government through its paces. Perhaps he had spoken only from a wishful thought, for he, too, must be hoping that this would be over soon.

It was no surprise to her that he felt that way—but to have it stated so plainly had been like a hard slap across her face. He hadn't so much as touched her all weekend, since that one instant in the car when they had first arrived. Sometimes, it seemed to her that he was going out of his way to avoid her, as if the mere brush of her hand would be repulsive. In the meantime, her very soul ached for his touch.

She had worked for him for two years, but he would never have noticed her at all if it hadn't been for this idiotic notion of Russell Glenn's. Remember that,

Gayle, she told herself fiercely. She would be some kind of fool to allow herself to think any differently

She huddled a blanket around her shoulders and sat on the love seat in front of the empty fireplace in her bedroom. For the first time, she began to think seriously of what she would do when this bogus engagement was finished. A different job? Elizabeth had said Gayle could easily get a job in Chicago——

No. To remain friends with Elizabeth would be to hear too much of Jared. Elizabeth would know each piece of gossip, the name of each new woman, and Gayle would be weak enough to ask her to repeat it. It would be better if she didn't know—better to cut herself off completely, rather than to fret over each detail of what he was doing.

She must keep going, that was sure. She must not let this loss paralyse her, as for so many years she had been immobilised by Craig's death. But in what direction would she go?

Her dream once, had been to become an accountant. Was it too late to pursue that? Darrel had seemed to think that she could still do anything she wanted. Perhaps if she could live very inexpensively, and go to school—She had some money saved to help her through . . .

She tumbled off into exhausted sleep, and dreamed of tax forms and audits. But it was Jared's name she saw on all the papers, and in her sleep the tears crept down her cheeks.

On Monday morning, Gayle woke to silence, and panic, for Amy was not in the room. Her small bed was empty, the blankets pushed back, and the glass door was partly open. If she had gone out to play in the courtyard, and tumbled into the pool——

Gayle hurried into her robe, fear making her fingers clumsy on the buttons. But as she reached the courtyard, the sound of a high, childish voice drew her on to the dining room. She paused in the doorway just as Amy sneaked a link sausage from Jared's plate.

'The little thief has eaten half my breakfast,' he complained, and Amy giggled. 'I think I've ruined her peanut butter habit.'

'Rachel will be eternally grateful for that.' Gayle wrapped her hands around a mug of hot coffee. Though the room was pleasantly warm, she needed the comfort provided by the warm cup.

Peters had come in on silent feet. 'What would you like this morning, Miss Bradley?'

'Just coffee. Thanks, Peters.'

'You've broken his heart,' Jared observed. 'He thinks you don't like his cooking.'

'That's silly. I'm just not very hungry this morning.'

'With all the concentrated hours of work this weekend, I'd think you'd be starving.' He pushed his plate back and refilled his cup. 'Can you and Amy be ready to leave in an hour?

Her eyes went automatically to the window wall and to the lush greenery in the courtyard beyond. This is the last time, she thought. I will not pass this way again. Never again to walk along the flagstone paths, never again to watch the fire crackle on the hearth in that lovely bedroom, never again to pet Underdog's soft coat——

'Where did you get the dog?' she asked. 'You never did tell me.'

'From my brother. Right after I gave his son a mynah bird.'

Gayle said judiciously. 'You should be grateful that he restrained himself.'

'I know. I expected a pair of monkeys at least. I think the Yorkie was intended to make me feel ridiculous.' He reached across the table to take her hand, then stopped before he touched her as if his fingers had crashed into a wall. There was a long silence. 'Gayle——' he said finally.

She waited, holding her breath. But he said only, 'I want to get those documents filed this morning,' and Gayle suddenly realised that she had not answered his question.

'We'll be ready in any hour,' she said quietly.

His eyes flicked across her, and then, without a word, he rose and left the room.

Gayle ran a hand over her hair. It was still tangled from sleep; she had been too anxious to find Amy to bother with a brush. No wonder he'd walked out, she thought. She was no lovely sight to share a breakfast table with, that was certain.

She was very quiet on the way back to Denver. Jared didn't seem to notice her moodiness; Amy was keeping him entertained with her constant questions and chatter.

Gayle, when she could get her mind off her own troubles, was intrigued. The one thing she would never have expected was that Jared would treat the child as anything but a nuisance. Instead, he had spent hours with her.

Certain people, Gayle thought, would have been very shocked by that . . .

They stopped in front of the little house in the suburbs, and Jared waited in the car while she took Amy back to her mother. Gayle made an excuse to Rachel, promising insincerely that of course she would invite him to dinner on Friday. Part of her hoped that by Friday she would be free once more—and the other part of her hoped just as fervently that Friday would never come.

Living in this confusion was like walking through an endless dream, she thought. None of it was real, none of it made sense. Each day was just another scene in the haze, to be survived. Eventually she would wake up.

'Russell Glenn is coming into the office this morning,' Jared said as the lift creaked towards the executive floor. 'I want to see him the minute he shows up. And I don't want to be interrupted by anything.' He absently tapped the Liberty dollar set in his ring against the door, as if he could force the lift to speed up.

Gayle nodded, and tried to drown her irritation at the rhythmic banging. He probably wasn't even aware that he was doing it, she thought. In the old days, it wouldn't have bothered her; a professional secretary didn't let her employer's little habits get to her . . .

Jared hurried off the elevator as soon as it stopped, and tripped over a crate that had been left by the door. He swore, and said, 'What is this thing doing here?'

Gayle glanced at the label, and knew. 'It's Elizabeth again,' she said, with deep certainty.

The man who was waiting patiently outside the executive suite gave her a toothy smile and a business card. 'Miss Bradley? I'm from the Harrington Galleries, and I'm delighted to deliver this painting for you. We tried to contact you over the weekend to see where you'd like it delivered——'

'Did you charge this to my credit card, too?' Jared asked.

'I didn't buy it at all,' Gayle said defensively.

'This should clear everything up,' the gallery man said smoothly, and put a large cream-coloured envelope into Gayle's hand.

She tore it open. The card inside said, in copper-plate script, 'For Miss Gayle Bradley, with the love and best wishes of Mr and Mrs Whitney Logan.'

'I take it back,' she said. 'It wasn't Elizabeth—at least not directly.' She gave Jared the card.

He read it and groaned. 'Now my mother is getting into the act!'

'Five million people read that magazine every week, Jared,' she snapped, her temper goaded past any kind of control. 'It's a little unrealistic to expect your mother not to have heard about your engagement!'

'Miss Bradley,' the gallery man said again, 'where would you like me to put this?'

An answer trembled on her lips, but Gayle swallowed it. 'You might as well bring it into the office and uncrate it,' she said finally.

Jared flung the gift card on to her desk, and turned at the door of his own office. 'Gayle, call Russell Glenn's hotel—make sure he didn't forget our appointment.'

'Of course.' She didn't know what he planned to do, but all too obviously this gift had been the last straw. It made no sense, she thought. How could he have expected to keep his parents in the dark, when he'd notified absolutely everyone? He had laughed everything else—but an art gallery crate had held no humour for him at all.

She reached for the 'phone just as the gallery man took the painting out of the crate. As she had expected, it was the seascape. Under the bright office lights, the crisply curling waves glared white as they smashed themselves into foam against the rocky shore. But under more gentle lighting, she knew, the painting would be a misty blue late afternoon, or a plum twilight.

She stared into the depths of the canvas, only half listening as the gallery man told her about the painter's methods, his expertise, his brushwork. All that would have been fascinating had she been the owner of this painting, she thought. But as it was, she would just consider it a rental from a museum somewhere . . .

Russell Glenn came in before the gallery man was finished with his art appreciation course, and she waved him on into Jared's office. She tried to occupy herself with her own work, all the things which had been put off last week because of the party for the new computer, and the Softek deal. But her hands were shaking and her mind was on the two men behind that closed door. What were they saying to one another in there?

It's my future, too, she wanted to scream. I should have a voice in it!

She looked down at the padparadschah ring on her

hand. That's funny, she thought. I never noticed before that it looks like an eye—a sinister orange pupil surrounded by sparkling eyelashes. An evil eye.

The chime of the telephone pulled her away from her fascinated contemplation of the gem.

'Mr Logan's office,' she said.

'Gayle? This is Larry.'

She hadn't talked to him in two weeks. Oh, God, she thought, this is all I need this morning.

'Darrel told me you're engaged,' he said quietly. 'I just wanted to give you my best wishes.'

Her heart twisted a little. Under other circumstances, she thought, might Larry have been more than just a pest? If she hadn't still been convinced, when she met him, of her undying love for Craig—if she hadn't become embroiled in this awful mess with Jared—might she have eventually come to care for Larry?

Too late, now, she told herself. Once in love with Jared, there was no room left for anyone else. And even if Jared went out of her life, he would never entirely leave her heart.

She thanked Larry, somehow. She knew there was a catch in her voice, and she blotted a tear off her eyelashes after she cradled the 'phone.

Russell Glenn left an hour later, just as cheerful as ever. Jared leaned silently against the door jamb, his face unrevealing, until Russell was out of sight. Then he broke into a boyish grin and stretched, as if every muscle in his body suddenly cried out for the release of tension.

'Come on in, Gayle,' he said. 'This calls for a celebration!'

She took her usual chair in his office, hoping that the sudden drumming of her heart wasn't loud enough for him to hear. 'What happened?' she asked.

He turned from the bar, holding the bottle of champagne that had been left over from their late-night supper. 'Russell finally signed the papers.' He popped the cork with an expert twist, and poured two glasses full. He handed one to Gayle and dropped into his leather chair, holding the other. 'He finally signed the contract to sell Softek!'

'How did you manage that?' She kept her voice even and quiet. Did he have to sound quite so happy about it? she thought raggedly.

'I told him that I was going to a lot of expense and effort here without any commitment on his part, and I threatened to call off the deal today unless he signed the agreement to sell.'

He was so unhappy, she thought, that he would even have sacrificed Softek to get rid of me—to get out of this awful trap. The very thing he wanted so badly a few weeks ago, he had been ready to give up this morning.

'Don't you see, Gayle?' He was leaning forward. 'It's over. He has to sell the company now—he can't back out! The government can take as long as it likes, now—it doesn't matter!'

'It's over,' she repeated. She felt dazed. She raised the glass and sipped her champagne. It tasted like mouthwash.

'Russ and Krystal are going back to California tomorrow. I told Russell we'd have dinner with them tonight——'

She pictured the four of them at the Pinnacle. Could she stand to do that, she wondered, to sit there beside him and pretend one more time, when she knew in every cell of her body that she would never be with him again?

'No,' she said. It was only a breath.

He frowned. 'What do you mean—no?'

She didn't answer. She set the tulip glass down on the corner of his desk. Her hand wasn't even trembling as she reached for her notebook and pencil. 'Where do we begin?'

'What the devil are you talking about, Gayle?'

'If it's over, then there is no more need for this farce. I'll start on a list of people to notify.'

He set his glass down with a bang. 'To notify of what?'

Gayle raised an eyebrow. 'That we are no longer engaged, of course. People are calling with congratulations—I'm sure it's a bit embarrassing for you. You'll want to call your parents first, of course, and let them know.'

'You aren't wasting any time, are you?'

She met his eyes for the first time. 'I see no need to delay things. What about Elizabeth? Do you want to break the news to her or shall I?'

There was a long silence. Then Jared said, very quietly, 'I'll tell her.'

'I'll have to call Darrel, of course,' Gayle mused. 'Before the break-up gets the coverage that the engagement did.'

'Russell Glenn is going to think this is very strange.'

Gayle raised an eyebrow. 'I thought it didn't matter any more,' she pointed out gently. She made some meaningless marks on her notebook. 'Too bad I had that painting uncrated. The man could just as well have taken it back with him.'

'Take it back? Why? It was a gift!'

'A gift intended for your fiancée. Which I no longer am.'

His voice was low. 'I'll call the gallery and take care of the painting.'

'Will you? Thank you. Please tell your mother that I——' She started to choke, swallowed hard, started over. 'Tell her that I appreciated the thought.' Tell her, she thought, that I would have loved to meet her—that I would have loved to be her daughter ... No. There was no time now for wishes like that. To dwell on things which would never be could only hurt her more.

She turned her hand slowly, and watched one last time as the padparadschah caught fire from the lights and sent it back to her in slivers. Then she slid the ring from her finger.

It's like losing my left arm, she thought, to have it gone. No, she told herself firmly. It's like being released from prison.

She leaned across the desk and put the ring gently down on the blotter. She didn't know what she would have done if he had reached for it; she could not have trusted herself to touch him, for fear of what she might do.

'It's yours,' he said. 'That was the deal.'

Gayle shook her head. 'I don't keep things that I didn't earn,' she whispered.

'You might as well have it. It has no meaning.'

And that's exactly why I'm returning it, she thought. It means all the world to me, and nothing to you. For one brief instant, she wished that she had thrown it at him.

But a professional secretary doesn't do things like that, she reminded herself. And that was all she was now. It was all she had left—her profession, and her pride.

'If you'll excuse me,' she said, 'I have work to do.'

'Gayle?' he said, and she turned at the door.

He picked up the ring and turned it over and over in his hand. She could almost see the flashes of orange, amber, green—she had watched the padparadschah perform so many times. Then he closed his hand over the ring, and looked up at her. 'It's really over, isn't it?' he said. His voice was so quiet that she almost didn't hear.

She forced herself to smile. You're happy, Gayle, she reminded herself. 'Yes, Mr Logan,' she said gently. 'It's all over.'

CHAPTER TWELVE

GAYLE pulled a letter from the printer and read it quickly, certain that she had finally got it right. Then she saw the misspelling that had escaped her eye on the computer screen. In a fit of temper, she crumpled the page and threw it at the nearest wastebasket. This would be the third set of corrections she'd done, and Gayle was tired. She wanted to just sit down and cry.

A glance at the clock didn't help. It was only the middle of the afternoon, and she felt as if she'd been in the office for ten days straight.

It had been, she thought, the longest ten days of her life, since that Monday morning when she had wrenched the padparadschah ring off her finger. Since then, whenever the intercom buzzed or Jared's office door opened, Gayle jumped. She was growing afraid of shadows, too, she noted grimly. And she kept making foolish mistakes—stupid things that not even the most inexperienced girl in the secretarial pool would do. It was enough to drive a professional secretary to drink— or to find a new career.

It had been ten days of agony. He'd gone to dinner that Monday night with Russ and Krystal Glenn; Gayle herself had reserved the table. She didn't know if he had told them the truth or given them some excuse for her absence, and she didn't care. She had stayed at home, forced herself to eat a carton of yoghurt left over from Amy's stay, and cried.

It had not got easier. The speculation in the papers about their shattered romance was bad enough, but Jared seemed to be purposely fuelling it. She didn't know which women he was seeing, but she had booked his favourite table for two at The Pinnacle on a half dozen evenings. He was coming into the office late in the mornings, looking tired, as if his evening's entertainment had lasted far into the night. He seemed to be trying to make up for lost time, she thought bitterly—time he had wasted on her.

She made the necessary corrections on her letter, holding on to the shreds of her patience. Tasks that two months ago she would have welcomed because they required little thought now bored her to extinction, leaving her wanting to scream. That was what was wrong with this job, she concluded—there was to much time to think. And far too many things to think about.

She knew that she should quit. She had to get away, or one of these days she'd just tune her brain to a broadcast no one else could hear, and she'd wander out the rest of her life in a private little daze like Ophelia. The really frightening thing was that she didn't care.

Dammit, she told herself angrily. You'd think you would have learned something from all those years of moping over Craig! But this was different . . .

She reached for the chiming telephone, and her white cuff—a sharp contrast to the black of ther dress— caught against a ball-point pen, sending a streak of midnight blue ink across the linen, Damn, she thought. It was the sort of thing that would never have happened to the old Gayle—the professional one.

'Mr Logan's office,' she said, trying to get just the right tone back into her voice.

'Gayle—what's this about you refusing to have lunch with us next week?' It was brisk, no nonsense.

Gayle sighed. 'Hello, Elizabeth.'

'Helene called me a few minutes ago to read me your civil little note. Cold, I call it.'

'It was the only thing I could do,' Gayle pointed out. 'She wrote me that letter before she knew the engagement had been broken. The invitation to lunch was issued to Jared's fiancée, and I'm sure it would have been a embarrassment to us all if I had accepted it.'

'She's far from embarrassed. In fact, she's very disappointed.'

'I don't understand why she should be.' Gayle's voice was level.

'Gayle, every fisherman wants to get a glimpse of the one that got away. Give the woman a break——'

'I am not having lunch with Jared's mother, Elizabeth.'

'Look at it this way.' Elizabeth's tone was sweetly reasonable. 'Wouldn't you rather sit in a restaurant with a cup of coffee and a chicken salad croissant—and me for moral support—than to have her drop in unannounced at the office?'

'She wouldn't do that.' Then, hesitantly, 'Would she?'

Elizabeth laughed. 'Frankly, I wouldn't bet on what Helene will do. Someday I'll tell you about the first time I met her. If you take my advice——'

Gayle sighed. 'Taking your advice is what got me into this mess. His credit card bill was in this morning's mail, by the way.'

'Oh?' Elizabeth sounded mildly interested. 'How big was it?'

'I didn't open it.'

'You have no nerve, Gayle.' There was a long silence. Then the tone of Elizabeth's voice changed. 'This is not a joke any more, is it?'

'It's never been screamingly funny, Elizabeth.'

'Is he being beastly?'

No, Gayle thought, and that makes it even worse. If he was being irritable, or angry, or unfair, or demanding—I could take it, because at least then I could let myself believe that it was bothering him as much as it is me. But it hasn't made a difference—any difference at all. It's just as it used to be. He doesn't even know I'm here—he treats me like one of his damned computers! The efficient Miss Bradley . . .

'Tell him I put you up to buying the clothes,' Elizabeth urged. 'Surely he won't blame you——'

Suddenly she had to get off the 'phone, away from that sympathetic voice, before she burst into tears. 'I have to go.'

'All right. We'll be flying in next Friday, so I'll see you then, whether you decide to have lunch with us or not.'

Not if I have anything to say about it, Gayle thought. It wasn't that she didn't want to see Elizabeth, but she knew that those intelligent green eyes would need only moments to diagnose what was wrong with Gayle. And that, she knew, she could not bear. She had probably said too much already.

So, next week when the Logans came to Colorado to ski, Gayle Bradley would be very careful where she went. If necessary, she would even come down with a cold and stay at home all week—with the telephone unplugged—until they were safely out of Denver.

She stared thoughtfully across the office, out over the city skyline, and wondered fearfully what Jared would have to say about the credit card bill. He hadn't seen it yet; she had waited till he'd gone out to the factory before putting it on his desk. She almost hoped that he'd be late getting back, so she could be gone before the explosion hit.

But there was no explosion. He came in and went to his office without a word to Gayle. And though she bit a fingernail down to the quick while she waited, the intercom remained silent.

Perhaps it doesn't matter, she concluded finally. Perhaps it was worth the cost to him, now that he doesn't have the engagement—and me—around his neck anymore . . .

Rachel came in a bare half-hour before quitting time. She had Amy with her, bundled into a yellow snowsuit.

'What brings you downtown?' Gayle asked lightly.

Rachel smiled. 'I know it's harder for you to say no

in person than over the phone,' she confided. 'So I come in to ask you—no, to TELL you—that Darrel and I are taking you to dinner tonight as a thank-you for keeping Amy last weekend.'

'That's sweet, but you don't need to——'

'We want to. We'll pick you up at seven.'

Gayle didn't have the energy to argue. 'All right,' she said, and Rachel rewarded her with a smile.

Jared's office door opened. 'Gayle, I'm going home early. Did you make my dinner reservations?'

'Have I ever forgotten them?' She could not keep the bitter tone from her voice.

He looked at her for a long moment, and then stooped to pick up Amy, who was tugging at his hand.

'Uncle Jared! Uncle Jared!' she was chanting.

'Well, what is it, brat?' he teased.

There was an impish sparkle in her eyes. 'Take me to the zoo,' she demanded.

'Amy!' Her mother stepped forward to take the child.

Jared smiled as he handed her back. 'You belong in the zoo with the rest of the monkeys,' he told Amy, a fingertip caressing the dimple at the corner of her mouth.

A smile for Rachel, a caress for Amy. And for Gayle—'Call Peters,' he said from the doorway. 'Tell him I'll be at Pino Reposo for the weekend.'

For me, not even a goodbye, Gayle thought wearily.

The early winter dark had dropped over the city when she left the Logan building on her way to the bus stop. Tonight, she thought, she would wear one of the dresses she'd brought with Jared's credit card. There was one the precise colour of the padparadschah. It would be the first time she would wear it—and the last. For tonight would be her farewell to him—the first step in putting this whole horrible incident behind her. It would not be easy, and it would not be quickly done—but tonight she would begin.

She stepped into the doorway of the little gallery.

Partly it was a desire for shelter from the wind that sent
her there; partly a wish to once again study that lovely
seascape. She had visited it every day, as if she were
making a holy pilgrimage. What a perfect gift idea it
had been, she thought. Bless Elizabeth for the thought,
and Helene Logan for the act. She would have liked to
know them both better.

'And that is the kind of wishful thinking that you
have to get rid of,' she lectured herself under her breath.
'Stop it right now!'

The gallery window was dim. The painting would
look like twilight, under that subdued lighting. Perhaps,
Gayle thought, if she got another job right away, she
could buy it. She could have it stored in the gallery's
vault until she could pay it all off, and then it would be
hers to study and lose herself in every day . . .

But the painting wasn't in the window. In its place
was a still-life of flowers in a brass bowl.

It felt like a very important part of her was gone.
Gayle bit her lip, hard, and fought back the tears. How
silly to cry over a painting, she told herself fiercely,
when she had lost so much more than that.

She traced her steps slowly to the bus stop, and rode
home in a blue silence.

The evening had been a disaster from the start, she
concluded the next morning. How, she wondered, could
it have gone so wrong?

She had started out with good intentions. She would
be pleasant, she would have fun, she would be an
enjoyable companion. Then Rachel arrived with the
announcement that Darrel and Larry were waiting in
the car. 'I'm going to kill him,' she said. 'I had nothing
to do with it, Gayle, I swear——'

Gayle had burst into laughter, shocking both of
them, and said that nothing could make any difference.

What had happened certainly hadn't been Larry's
fault. He had treated her as if she were made of spun

glass. Perhaps that was why the evening had gone sour. At any rate, Gayle told herself, the mood had been fragile, and any enjoyment had been gone long before they reached the new little nightclub, and the maitre d' showed them to the table next to Jared Logan's.

That would have been bad enough. But to see Natalie Weston beside him, her hand possessive on his sleeve, her eyes challenging as she met Gayle's, had been the last straw.

Gayle didn't know how she had managed it, but she had smiled sweetly at them, chosen a chair that let her keep her back turned, and sipped a glass of wine, carrying on a brittle, cheery conversation with Larry, of which she remembered not one word. A few minutes later, Jared and Natalie had left the club.

With the whole city of Denver to choose from, Gayle had been thinking, they had ended up at adjoining tables, as if some evil genie was playing with them and taking delight in their discomfort.

They'd taken her home, and Rachel, worried, had offered to stay the night. Gayle had forced a smile and told her not to fret, that she wasn't going to do anything crazy. Her nerves were screaming for some time alone, some quiet, some peace to think.

Finally, reluctantly, Rachel had gone. Gayle had spent the night drinking coffee and listing her options. Eventually she had concluded that she had only one. No matter what else she did, she had to stop causing herself anguish. To do that, she must quit her job and go somewhere that she need never hear of Jared Logan again.

The late dawn was breaking when, her decision made, she ran a tub of bubbles and tried to soak the tension away. Then, for the last time, she dressed carefully in her self-imposed black uniform, put her hair up in the careful coil at the back of her neck, and walked down to the bus stop.

The winter sun was bright against the snow, and the

polished brass of the Logan building's doorway gleamed. She paused for a moment to study it, for she knew she would never again see it quite like this.

Then she sighed—it was a little silly to get sentimental about a chunk of brass, after all. She walked through the revolving door into the marble lobby, and ran headlong into Natalie Weston.

'Please watch where you're going, Gayle.' Natalie was crisp and fresh this morning in a bright plaid coat and matching tam. Over her shoulder was slung a leather model's bag. There was plenty of room in it, Gayle thought wryly, for her black lace negligée, and whatever else a girl needed for a night in the love nest . . . Or had Natalie, too, borrowed the red silk pyjamas?

'You have my sympathy, actually,' Natalie purred. 'It wasn't very tactful of Jared last night to just get up and walk out like that, was it? I'm afraid it will probably hit the papers.'

Gayle tried to ignore the venom in the woman's voice.

Natalie went on, 'You poor girl. One night in the love nest, and suddenly it was all over. How embarrassing it must be, to be rejected like that.' Her eyes flicked over Gayle. 'Of course,' she said thoughtfully, 'it could have been expected. One really can't blame Jared, of course . . .'

Gayle turned away and walked across the lobby, the haunting tinkle of Natalie's laughter following her.

Thomas looked sympathetic. 'Don't mind her,' he said. 'She doesn't mean anything to Mr Logan—I'll bet on it.' But his voice lacked conviction.

Gayle thought about saying. That's just it, Thomas. We don't any of us mean anything to Mr Logan. But instead she forced herself to smile, as if it didn't matter to her what Jared Logan did.

For the last time, she stood just inside the door of the office suite and watched the sunlight play over downtown Denver. For the last time, she made coffee in his office, and sharpened his pencils to the needle points he liked, and straightened the blotter the barest quarter of an inch.

'You're early this morning, Gayle.'

The voice was low, but firm. Jared was standing in the doorway, his arms folded across his chest, his shoulder propped against the jamb.

'I have a lot of things to do, Mr Logan,' she said quietly. She moved around the desk to her usual chair and sat down, her notebook ready for his instructions.

'Why are you calling me Mr Logan again?'

'It's more comfortable for me.' Should she tell him now that she was quitting, she wondered. No; she would wait till afternoon and give him her resignation letter. There would be less time for questions that way.

He sat down behind his desk and flipped through the stack of mail. 'You'd better call Peters again and check on the last-minute arrangements for next week at Pino Reposo.'

'Very well,' she said, keeping her voice steady with an effort. I could have been there, she thought. I could have been his hostess . . .

'And call the flower shop downstairs, please. Have them send a dozen red——'

'No.'

He raised an eyebrow. 'What did you say?'

'I said no.' She hadn't intended to make a fuss about this, but sending flowers to Natalie Weston today would be more than she could bear. 'No more dinner reservations, no more flowers sent to your overnight guests. That isn't part of my job, so if you want those things done, you'll have to take care of them yourself.'

He put the mail aside and leaned back in his chair, tenting his fingertips together.

'In case you're thinking of firing me,' she said, trying to keep her voice from trembling, 'you needn't. I quit. You'll have my letter of resignation just as soon as I can type it.' She reminded herself that he must not know how painful this was for her.

He stroked his moustache. The gold coin on his finger gleamed. 'I assume that you're giving the customary four week's notice?'

'No.' He hadn't even tried to talk her out of it. It was no more than she had expected, but it still hurt. Her voice was ragged now. 'Four minutes notice is all I'm willing to give you.' She tossed the notebook down on the corner of his desk and stood up. 'You'd better call the secretarial pool right now if you want someone up here by the time I'm ready to leave.'

She paused in the outer office long enough to seize her handbag and her coat. No time for a farewell glance at her favourite view, no time to pick up those few personal items that had crept into her desk over the months. She had about two minutes before the tears would overwhelm her, and she was determined to be out of the building before that happened.

God, she thought as she ran for the lift, how I hate this. I feel like a wet tissue most of the time—either fighting off tears or mopping up after them . . .

Thomas was startled to see her. 'Miss Bradley!' he called across the lobby after her. 'Is something wrong?'

She didn't bother to answer. I must get outside, she thought. Once I'm out in the cold——

Then Jared's voice rang throught the lobby, echoing against the marble. 'Gayle!' It was like a whip, lashing across her sensitive ears. 'Damn it, Gayle, come back here or I will have you arrested for forging my name on those credit card slips!'

She paused in the door. 'You can't do it. You authorised me to use that card!'

'Not to buy out every clothing store in Denver, I didn't!'

He won't do it, she thought. It would be embarrassing, and his ego is already bruised . . . But her momentary hesitation was a fatal mistake.

His hand closed on her arm, and he said, with grim satisfaction, 'Let's go back upstairs and discuss this.'

'No!' She struggled, and he swore as her toe connected with his shin. He finally picked her up bodily and carried her across the lobby. 'Now I know where Amy got her temper,' he said coolly. 'Hold that lift for us, Thomas.'

'Don't you dare, Thomas!' Gayle threatened.

If the whole thing hadn't been so awful, she'd have laughed at Thomas' expression. He shifted from one foot to the other, and finally said apologetically, 'You said it yourself, Miss Bradley. He's the one who signs my paycheques,' as he held the lift door.

She made a grab for the buttons, and Jared caught her hand. 'Take your choice, Gayle,' he said. 'We can go upstairs and talk about this quietly, just the two of us—or we can finish it as it was started, down in the lobby, with the world listening in. But we will discuss it. Which is it going to be?' There was no hint of humour in his voice, and he took her silence for assent.

But when the lift door opened, she took one look into the hallway and wailed. 'Can't we go to the office?'

'There will be no interruptions here.' He unlocked the door of the penthouse apartment and ushered her inside without a hint of gentleness in his manner.

She stood in the hall, her hands deep in the pockets of her coat, and shook her head when he tried to take it. 'I don't plan to stay long,' she pointed out.

'Suit yourself.' He kept a hand on her elbow until they were in the living room. Then, with a thoughtful look at her, he touched a series of buttons on the control panel by the couch. 'Now,' he said. 'I'll get you a cup of coffee, if you promise not to throw it at me.' He tossed his jacket across the ledge and pulled his tie loose.

'Aren't you afraid I'll run?' she asked, defiantly. 'What did you do, lock me in?'

'No—but I reprogrammed the burglar alarm. If that

door is opened, half the Denver police force will be surrounding the building by the time you get to the lobby.'

That was an out-and-out lie, she thought. On the other hand, it sounded like the kind of thing an electronics wizard like him might have worked out. She wasn't about to test it, that was sure.

Too restless to sit still, she followed him into the tiny stainless steel kitchen. Instantly, she regretted it, as he reached around her to get the cups. She stepped back with a quick apology.

'Dammit, would you stop cringing away from me?' he said, his voice sharp. 'I'm not going to hit you—any more than I'd kick Underdog for getting in my way.'

'Sorry.'

'And stop apologising!'

She bit her lip and maintained an icy silence until the coffee was poured. Then she said, stiffly, 'Why did you follow me down to the lobby? If I hadn't quit you would have fired me—so why did you bother to come after me?'

'What makes you think I'd have fired you? Come to that, what made you quit?'

'Come on, Jared. You were ready to sacrifice the Softek deal entirely rather than have me messing up you life any more.'

'On the contrary. I wouldn't have given it up. I pulled a bluff—and Russell Glenn didn't call it.' He took a long swallow from his cup. 'I was planning to offer you a promotion, Gayle. As soon as the Softek purchase is final, I want my own people in there. If you'd like the job of running that division——'

He was very anxious to get her out of the office, she thought. But—if that was so—why hadn't he just let her go this morning?'

'No, thanks,' she said stiffly. 'I don't want Krystal's job. In any case, you don't need to buy me off. Mr Logan. I'll go quietly.'

'Why are you so anxious to leave?' Over the rim of his cup, his eyes were deep blue. The question was silky, and she let the silence drag out while she fumbled for an answer that he would accept. She wondered what he would do if she said, I fell in love with you . . .

'Do you have a new job waiting for you?' he prompted. 'A new challenge? Working for Larry, perhaps? That was him you were with last night, wasn't it?'

'Yes,' she admitted. 'It was Larry. And no, I'm not going to work for him. I might go back to school,' she said finally.

He set his cup down, and his eyes were cold and hard. 'You don't have the least idea what you're going to do, do you?' he asked. 'And you also don't want to talk about it. Well, I can explain it, since you're not going to.'

'To tell you the truth,' she said, goaded beyond endurance, 'I don't care what I do as long as I get away from you.'

'That's at least the approximate truth, Gayle. You're not comfortable working for me any more because the mere sight of me reminds you that your ordered little world has been turned upside down, and your devotion to a dead man has been challenged.'

'I loved Craig,' she said automatically.

'And now you're trying to hide behind him again. The black dresses, the hairstyle—But you can't do it any more, Gayle. You can run from me, but you can't hide from the truth about yourself.'

'What truth do you think you've discovered, Jared?'

'I know that under the frozen shell there is still a woman, alive and vital and passionate. I didn't set out to find her, but I brought her back to life—and I'm proud of it.'

'Oh, you have a lot to be proud of,' she stormed, unable any longer to keep her temper in check. 'You're not only the world's greatest lover, but you're greedy, conceited, opinionated the all-time champion egotistical son of a——'

He was smiling. 'That proves my point, doesn't it? The old Gayle Bradley would never have spouted off at me like that. She'd have given me that little Mona Lisa smile that said I was just being silly. You've changed, Gayle—and putting on the old black dress won't make you the person you used to be.'

The kitchen was suddenly too small for Gayle. She slammed her cup down on the counter-top and turned to leave the room.

'I don't blame you for wanting out,' he said. 'It hasn't been a pleasant few weeks for either of us. But don't go, Gayle. Please—don't leave me.'

'You need a secretary, right?' Her voice was bitter.

'No. I need you.' He had spoken so softly that she thought for an instant that she might have imagined it. 'The engagement started out as a nuisance, and ended up as a habit—a pleasant habit, Gayle. You're—restful to be with.'

'Gee, thanks.' She supposed that he had meant it as a compliment. But she was certain that he'd never told Natalie Weston that she was restful!

'At first the whole thing was sort of a joke. I found it humorous that you preferred your memories of Craig to me. Then it became a challenge to make you see that you were wasting your life. And then——'

'People quit smoking every day, Jared. If they can kick cigarettes, you can get along without me.'

She stopped in the doorway of the living room just as a stray shaft of light sparkled across the face of the painting that hung over the fireplace. Suddenly, in the seascape, it was early morning on a foggy day.

Confusion swept over her in a wave. He'd brought the painting here, she thought—but why? 'You sent it back to the gallery,' she said. 'I know you did, because I saw it there——' Her coat dropped unnoticed into a heap on the carpet, and Gayle leaned on the low wall behind the conversation pit, her eyes on the painting. Then she turned to look at him. 'Why did you bring it here?'

'It seemed to belong here.' He was a good eight feet from her, as if afraid that to approach her too suddenly might frighten her away. 'As you belong here, Gayle.'

She shook her head, but the gesture held no vehemence. Why would he have hung the painting in his love nest? she wondered. Surely not for love of the work itself; it was beautiful, but not his style.

'I was going to give it to you, later,' he said. 'I will give you anything that is in my power to give, Gayle——'

'I can't be bought.' She turned her back on the painting, facing him defiantly. 'You have a lot of nerve,' she said. 'I met Natalie this morning on her way out of the building.'

'And you think she was up here,' he said.

'What else can I think?' Her arms were folded defensively across her chest. 'An hour later you were ordering flowers——'

'For a friend who's in the hospital.'

Gayle considered that, and shook her head. 'I don't believe you.'

'It's true. In the last ten days, I've taken half a dozen women to dinner. I tried to find that old enjoyment again, but all the time I was with them, I was thinking about you.' He half-smiled. 'You've ruined my carefree bachelor life, Gayle.'

For how long, she wondered. Until I've slept with him?

'And I came back here every night alone,' he added. 'I was bored with them—as I have never been bored with you.'

'I'm nothing special,' she muttered.

'But you are. Oh, I tried to tell myself you were like all the rest. When the credit card bill came yesterday I almost had myself convinced. Ten thousand dollars worth of clothes makes quite a trousseau.'

'Ten thousand——' Her voice was panicky.

'Elizabeth taught you well. But then there was the matter of the ring. Any other woman would have kept it. You——' He stopped, and then went on harshly. 'You didn't want it.' He pulled one hand from his pocket, and there in his palm sparkled the padparad-schah.

Gayle's head was spinning. She had spent that much money in an afternoon's spree? My God, she thought, how will I ever pay it back?

'You broke our engagement——'

'I called a halt to a stupid prank!' she said.

He ignored the interruption. '—because of a man who's been dead for seven years, Gayle.'

But you're the one who wanted it to be over, she thought.

'I know you loved him, Gayle,' he said finally. 'But he's dead! Don't climb into the grave after him!'

She started to speak, and he silenced her with an upraised hand. 'All I'm asking for is a chance, Gayle— the opportunity to show you that you can still be happy without him. It isn't disloyal to look for happiness with someone else——' He broke off and rubbed a hand across the back of his neck. 'I'm making a muddle of this aren't I?'

'Yes,' she said. 'You are.'

'You see, I think you care just a little bit for me, Gayle, or you wouldn't respond to me the way you do. I think that down deep you know that you want me, too. It might not be the love you felt for Craig, but I don't care. I'll wait forever if I must, but I will not just stand by while you bury your heart with him. I will fight for you—I will do whatever it takes to wake you up——'

His fingers were probing the coil of hair at the back of her neck, searching out the pins and dropping them one by one on the carpet. 'That's better,' he said as her hair tumbled in loose curls around her face. 'That's my Gayle—with her hair down and her temper white-hot.'

There was strain in his eyes, but there was something else there too, a warmth she had never seen him display before. His voice held a new note, too, she thought—of fondness, affection ... Can this really be happening to me? she wondered.

'Gayle, give me another chance. Let me go back a month, a year, and start over—I want to wipe out all that foolishness and start fresh.'

'We can't go back, Jared.' She was weakening, and afterwards, she wondered, what then? How long would this madness of his last, before he was done with her?

'Let me show you the fun we can have together—there is something between us, Gayle. You can't deny that.' His hand lay gently against the curve of her throat. 'You can't pretend that your heart isn't pounding right now. And even if that something is purely sexual, it's a start.'

She closed her eyes, swaying against him, mesmerised by his sheer closeness. 'Why didn't you make love to me that night?' she murmured.

'It will sound silly,' he warned.

'I could stand a laugh right now!'

There was a long pause, then he said, 'Because I didn't want it to be the same with you as it always was with the other women. The first time we make love, Gayle——'

'You sound so certain that we will,' she mused. Had he told them all the same thing, she wondered.

'I am certain,' he said. 'In fifteen minutes I could have you in that bedroom begging me to make love to you.'

'So why don't you try it?' she asked, very softly.

He drew a long ragged breath. 'Because what I said wasn't quite true,' he admitted. 'I'm afraid, Gayle. Afraid that if I tried to seduce you, and you said no—I want you so badly that I'm not sure I could stop.'

The painful honesty left her breathless.

He mused, 'I used to think it was cute that my brother couldn't breathe easy when his wife was out of the room. Now I know what it's like to love someone so much that she is my life.'

There was no mistaking the torment in his voice, the agony, the despair. This was the man she had thought had no heart? Gayle reached out to him, blindly. 'Jared—please don't . . .'

He took her hand, and held it to his lips. 'When I finally fell in love,' he said. 'I had to do it the hard way.'

His words dropped into a sudden stillness in the room, and for an instant Gayle thought she was going to faint.

She turned absolutely white. His arm was around her in an instant, supporting her. 'I'm sorry,' he said. 'I shouldn't have said that. I didn't mean to shock you with it.'

'It isn't true,' she whispered. 'It can't be true.'

'Oh, but it is, my dear. I've never told any woman that, till now.'

Her voice was ragged. 'I don't believe you.'

'Gayle—you asked me once what I'd do if the woman I wanted was in love with another guy,' he said.

She thought about it. 'You laughed and said you'd probably punch him in the mouth,' she said unsteadily.

'That's right. Now I'm in that spot, and I can't go punch Craig because he's dead. And I'm stuck. I'm crazy in love—with a woman who loves a dead man—and I can't do anything about it.' He gave her a tiny shake. 'I won't push you, Gayle. I won't even tell you again that I love you, if that bothers you. I'll wait till you're ready to hear it.'

'You've never been known for patience.'

'I'll learn it,' he promised rashly. 'Just don't leave me.

Don't walk out on me. You see, Gayle, someday you might love me back,' he said. 'That's all I have to hold on to. Don't take that hope away from me.' He brushed a curl away from her face. 'I'll take whatever you're willing to give, and I swear I will be content with it.'

'What are you asking for, Jared?' I'll live with you, my love, she thought. But you must ask me . . .

'Ideally?' He laughed a little, as if at his own foolishness. 'You said once that being married to me was the worst fate you could imagine. I can accept that—I'm not much of a prospect as a husband. All I'm really asking is that you don't shut me out completely, Gayle.'

Gayle put her hands over her face. 'Oh, my God,' she whispered. 'Are you proposing to me?'

He nodded. 'I'd marry you this afternoon if that was what you wanted,' he said huskily. 'Or I'll wait forever, and count myself lucky every time I see you.'

She tried to speak, but her voice wouldn't work. Her throat was so tight that she could scarcely breathe. Finally, she whispered, 'Forever seems an awfully long way off.'

'I'll wait as long it takes, Gayle. Because I am certain that someday—I have to think that way. I couldn't bear it if there was no hope . . .'

'On the other hand,' she mused, 'I haven't a thing to wear to a wedding this afternoon. I'll have to go shopping. So what about next week, when your family is in town?'

The shock in his eyes frightened her for an instant. Had it all been a hoax? Had he been so confident that she would refuse him?

Then he was holding her so tightly that she could scarcely catch her breath. 'Gayle, I promise you,' he said, 'you will never have cause to regret this——'

'I've had an awful ten days, too,' she murmured. 'You were so anxious to get out of that engagement——'

He laughed, and held her tighter. 'At first, perhaps,' he admitted. 'To be honest, I didn't realise till after you'd given the ring back just how proud I was to have you wear it—to say that you were going to be my wife.' The platinum band was cool against her finger as he slid the padparadschah back where it belonged.

Gayle sighed contentedly and relaxed against him, feeling as if she'd finally come home.

'Gayle——' he said against her hair, his voice muffled. 'Craig must have been quite a guy. Someday—I think I'd like for you to tell me about him.'

His tone was almost humble. We can't have that, she thought. My arrogant Jared, feeling inferior?

'Craig was my first love,' she said quietly. 'I was a child then, and I made the mistake of thinking that first love was forever. And I kept making that mistake— until you straightened me out.'

He cupped her face in his hands and looked down into her eyes. 'Are you telling me not to be jealous of him?'

She nodded. 'No more than I am of your little black book.'

'I'll burn it,' he promised. Then he said, with a hint of laughter in his voice, 'Gayle, will you share my breakfast table?'

'Wherever you go, my love,' she said. 'Every morning of my life.'

He caught his breath at the glow in her eyes. 'If you keep looking at me like that,' he threatened, 'I'm tempted to take you back to the bedroom and teach one saucy young woman a badly needed lesson!'

She smiled. 'So teach me,' she said, very softly, and turned her face up to his.

Harlequin Presents

Coming Next Month

Available in May wherever paperback books are sold, or through Harlequin Reader Service.

In the U.S.
P.O. Box 1397
Buffalo, N.Y.
14240-1397

In Canada
P.O. Box 2800, Postal Station A
5170 Yonge Street
Willowdale, Ontario M2N 6J3

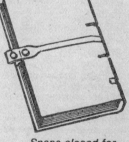

Take 4 novels and a surprise gift FREE